Praise for
Christmas is the Girl Next Door

"A gloriously sweet holiday read about expectations and reality."
—Kirkus Reviews

"A town called Christmas. An iffy wish come true. A new girl who could change it all. *All I Want For Christmas Is The Girl Next Door* kept me on my toes, turning pages from the start, and loving each revelation as it unfolded. Deep, funny, and real—this holiday romance will completely warm your heart and remind you that not all wishes should come true."
—Nova McBee, author of the *Calculated* Series

"Full of charm, wit, and so much warmth, Bobulski's *All I Want For Christmas Is The Girl Next Door* will have you breaking out in Christmas carols and will melt even the coldest heart!"
—Erin A. Craig, NYT Bestselling Author of *House of Salt and Sorrows*

"A cozy winter read you'll want to wrap yourself in like a blanket. At once bittersweet and hopeful, Bobulski thoughtfully explores the question of whether what we want is truly what we need against a backdrop of snowflakes, Christmas floats, and plenty of fresh cookies. A timeless holiday classic."
—Natalie Mae, author of *The Kinder Poison*

"This story is as magical as a shooting star on a cold winter night. Chelsea Bobulski's thoughtful and romantic exploration of true love and destiny will have readers swooning and wishing for her next Christmas novel!"
—Kristy Boyce, author of *Hot British Boyfriend*

"A fun frolic through the most wonderful time of the year! Full of heart and humor, this lighthearted twist on being careful what you wish for sparkles with delightful dialogue, swoony romance, and an ending that tugs at your heart before making it soar. Bobulski makes you think about being so focused on what we want that we miss what we already have. A holiday must-read!"
—Lori Goldstein, author of *Love, Theodosia, Sources Say*, and *Screen Queens*

"The charm of a small-town Hallmark Christmas meets the longing and wish fulfillment of John Green's *Paper Towns* in this magical holiday read. Expertly woven with strings of romance, ribbons of hope, and the sparkling power of gratitude, *All I Want For Christmas Is The Girl Next Door* is the perfect holiday story to curl up with on a snowy day. I adored every page!"
— Lorie Langdon, best-selling author of *Doon*, and *Olivia Twist*

"This is the book equivalent of drinking a mug of hot chocolate while listening to Christmas music as snowflakes gently fall outside. An all-around comforting, hopeful, and festive holiday read that will make you feel as cozy as your favorite Christmas movies."
—Kerry Winfrey, author of *Waiting for Tom Hanks*

All I Want For Christmas is

the boy i can't have

CHELSEA BOBULSKI

 WISE WOLF BOOKS LAS VEGAS

WISE WOLF
BOOKS

WISE WOLF BOOKS
An Imprint of Wolfpack Publishing

For information, address Wolfpack Publishing,
5130 S. Fort Apache Road, 215-380 Las Vegas, NV 89148
wisewolfbooks.com

Cover design by Wise Wolf Books

ISBN 978-1-953944-57-3 (paperback) 978-1-953944-56-6 (ebook)
LCCN: 2021947401

First Edition: December 2021

All I Want For Christmas is

the boy i can't have

To Nathan, for being better than every
romantic movie hero combined.

1

***

Mom is freaking out.

"You grabbed the *blue* folder, right?"

"Yes, Mom," I reply, cradling my cell against my ear as my rusty 1998 Pontiac Sunfire makes a left at the intersection, wheels squealing like a pig—not because I'm speeding (my driving instructor made me so terrified of getting a ticket that I refuse to drive over the speed limit even in an emergency like this) but because my car is basically an old, arthritic queen one pothole away from breaking down.

That's why I named her Bertha.

"Are you sure it's the blue one?" Mom asks, her voice frantic. "Because there was a purple one on my desk that in certain lighting can *look* blue—"

I glance at the folder in the passenger seat. It couldn't be more blue if it tried.

"Mom, calm down. It's the blue one, and I'm passing Cherry Street. I'll be there in two minutes."

Although it's October 25, with Halloween just around the corner, my hometown of Christmas, Virginia, is decked out in the same year-round yuletide decorations as it always is, with wreaths and twinkle lights looped around lampposts and instrumental Christmas jazz wafting through the outdoor speakers. The decorations will ramp up the closer we get to Christmas, but for now they're mixed with scarecrows on park benches and dried cornstalks on leaf-dusted stoops.

"No, no, no, the pink floral arrangement goes on the table with the bone china. The coral goes on the table with the pewter," Mom tells our new assistant, Daphne. She sighs into the phone, her voice less muffled as she turns back to me. "Just remember to—"

"Park that hunk of junk at the back entrance so the client doesn't see it," I say, reciting the order she gave me this morning. At the time, I rolled my eyes—what can I say? I'm protective of Bertha, and I always park in the back lot anyway—and, in the process, slopped cereal down the front of my very favorite Audrey Hepburn–inspired blouse.

Not a great start to a day that has only managed to get worse.

Case in point: I was *supposed* to drive straight to the office after school, giving me an hour to help Mom set up her big presentation, but then Mrs. Warren, my English teacher, stopped at my locker to see if I would tutor a freshman in *Romeo and Juliet*, which meant I ended up idling in the long line of cars trying to get out of the school parking lot, and then when I got to the office, Mom frantically scanned my empty hands.

"Where's the blue folder?" she asked.

"What blue folder?"

She pinched the bridge of her nose. "I left a voice mail on your phone thirty minutes ago asking you to pick it up on your way over here."

I tilted the face of my phone toward me so it would light up, and sure enough, there was a voice mail icon staring back at me. Oops. I raced home to retrieve the folder, only barely stopping myself from telling Mom to text next time—seriously, who pays attention to voice mail anymore?—and now I'm pulling onto Main Street, where Riddle Wedding Planning ("Wedding Starting to Feel Like a Riddle? We'll Solve It for You!") is located, with only five minutes to spare.

I turn into the back parking lot, the one reserved for all of the block's boutique shop employees, and drive up and down the rows, looking for a spot. Finally, I squeeze Bertha into an empty space that's not *technically* a space but not a fire lane either, grab the blue folder, turn off the ignition, and head inside.

Mom hasn't been leasing this office for very long—before this, she did all of her wedding planning out of our house—but it already feels like her. We painted the walls together, a soft gold ivory that's both clean and warm at the same time. Sienna photographs of the Eiffel Tower and cozy Paris streets line the walls. White votive and taper candles of varying sizes flicker throughout the room while the candles that smell like chocolate chip cookies burn out of sight. Our wedding dress shop (the business Mom started first, when I was still in diapers) sits in the old firehouse on the adjacent corner, in full view of the wedding planning office's front bay window.

I pass the open French doors leading to the staging area and spare a brief glance at Daphne, who's putting the finishing touches on miniature tables showcasing different wedding colors and reception themes, before heading into our conference room, which we purposefully decorated to look more like a cozy spot to have tea rather than a traditional conference room. Antique ivory couches sit facing each other with a long coffee table in between, topped with an autumn bouquet of roses, calla lilies, dried star flowers, and wheat stalks. We get a free bouquet delivery from Anselm's Flower Shop every week in exchange for working with them exclusively. The whole Anselm family pitches in to their business, and they're all incredibly talented—I'm talking *Vogue*-worthy flower arrangements.

Mom stands to the side of the couches, placing inspiration boards on easels. She turns to me as my flats slap the reclaimed hardwood floor.

"You can stop panicking," I say. "Blue folder is here."

"Oh, thank God." Her hands shake slightly as she takes the folder and rifles through the papers inside.

"Mom." I wrap an arm around her shoulder. "You're going to do great."

She exhales. "This is the biggest potential client we've ever had—"

"And if she doesn't choose us, it's her loss."

Mom gives me a half smirk, the kind that says she doesn't really believe me but she appreciates the attempt.

I try to stay calm for Mom's sake as we cover the inspiration boards with white damask cloths so that she can reveal each one individually, but now that I'm here, my hands start shaking too. A high-society bride doesn't come around a fairly new wedding planning business every day—especially one that, just over a year ago, was operating out of a three-bedroom ranch. If Kathleen Harker, daughter of the most sought-after criminal defense attorney in the state, chooses *us* to plan her big-budget wedding, it'll mean major exposure and the kind of paycheck that could cover our overhead for the next year, regardless of whether we get any more clients or not. Which isn't really a concern because if we impress Kathleen Harker and all of her single, aristocratic friends—also recently graduated from college and of marriageable age—we'll have brides banging down our door to work with us.

This could be the big break we've been praying for, and neither one of us wants to mess it up.

I set out a charcuterie plate while Mom arranges a variety of tea sandwiches and scones on a three-tiered cake stand that used to be a part of her own wedding china. Coffee and tea are poured into carafes, and Mom pops a bottle of champagne into the ice bucket just as the silver bells over the front door tinkle.

Daphne runs into the room, eyes wide. "They're here."

Mom lets out a long, slow breath.

I squeeze her hand as we step into the reception area to greet them.

The bride, a twenty-two-year-old blonde wearing a white dress under a fitted camel blazer, walks in first, followed closely by another blonde in an ivory pantsuit that looks like she could be her sister in a Botox-y kind of way. Next comes a man with short white hair, talking on his cell, and wearing a gold power tie that matches his cufflinks, and bringing up the rear is a boy who looks my age, but Mom strides forward to shake the bride's hand, blocking my view before I can get a good look at him.

"Welcome to Riddle Wedding Planning," Mom says, giving the bride and her family her warmest smile. There's no trace of the nervous energy that had been pulsing off of her a mere ten seconds ago. "This is my daughter, Isla, and my assistant, Daphne. It's our job to make your dream wedding a reality."

"Thank you," Kathleen replies, gazing around the room. Her Georgia-peach accent is the perfect replica of Scarlett O'Hara's. Odd for someone who grew up in Richmond. "I *love* your office. It's so much cozier than the others we've been to." The other blonde tugs on her arm. "Oh, excuse me. This is my mother, Maureen, and my father, Atticus."

"It's a pleasure to meet you," Mom says, shaking both of their hands as Atticus mumbles a hurried, slightly aggravated goodbye into his phone.

"And this," Kathleen continues, angling her body to the side and gesturing for the boy to come forward, "is my brother. August."

My heart stops.

Now, I'll admit, I am *not* the coolest cucumber around guys, especially cute ones with dimples and pushed back hair and stormy-gray eyes the *exact* same color as the bruised autumn sky outside. My best friends, Savannah Mason and Evelyn Waverley, say it's because I've been obsessed with fairy tales and One True Loves ever since I first watched *The Princess Bride* at the very impressionable age of six (but *come on*, how can anyone see the way Westley yearns for Buttercup and *not* want their own Dread Pirate Roberts whisking them away on a white horse?) and that the reason my brain goes numb and my tongue suddenly feels like it weighs a thousand pounds whenever I see a cute guy is because I instantly shift from thinking, *Oh, he's cute,* to *WHAT IF HE'S THE ONE?*

"You put so much pressure on yourself to be amazing and make a guy fall in love with you that you don't even act like yourself," Savannah told me once.

It would have hurt if it wasn't so true. I never come off well, but at least I've managed to form semi-coherent sentences around boys in the past. Probably because with other guys, the thought that they could be "the one" has always been a separate entity, a distant wonderment that makes me sit up and pay attention, just in case.

But now, I literally can't think of a *single* thing to say. My mind is completely and utterly blank as the rest of the world falls away, and for a brief, heart-stuttering moment, August stands in sharp relief against a fuzzy background of muted colors and shapes, the only clear, substantial thing in the entire room.

After taking in his hair (a darker shade of blond than his sister's, strands of gold mixed with wet sand) and the angles of his face—so sharp I could cut glass on his jaw and cheekbones—I zero in on his clothing. He's wearing trim, khaki dress pants; a crisp, white shirt with the sleeves rolled up to his elbows (exposing *gorgeously* tan forearms); and a blue tie emblazoned with a private-school emblem I don't recognize hanging loosely around his neck, as if pulling the knot down was the first thing he did the moment the last bell of the day rang.

He reaches his hand out, but all I can do is stare at it, taking in the gold hair dusting his knuckles and the little freckle on his thumb. I open my mouth to speak, but I can't remember what I'm supposed to say. There's a word for this. A greeting. Something you're supposed to say when you first meet someone.

Finally, it comes to me.

"HELLO," I shout, the word launching out of my mouth like a torpedo.

August's brows arch.

I stare at him.

He stares back.

And then I realize his hand is still stretched between us.

"Oh. Right." I slip my hand into his, suddenly aware of the millions of tiny nerve endings in my palm as his skin, smooth as cashmere, slides across my own.

"Nice to meet you," he says, his lips turning up slightly at the corners. The lilt in his words is pure Richmond, which makes me wonder if his sister is faking her accent. Then I remember Mom trying to work the University of Georgia's colors into the wedding theme, since that's where the bride and groom met. She must have picked up the accent there.

"You, too." The words slip through my lips on a breath.

His smile widens.

He lets go of my hand and the rest of the world comes back into focus, but it still feels like if I opened my mouth again, only a dull, static sound would emerge. Or maybe a guttural shriek.

Probably best to not say anything.

Mom has already led Kathleen and her parents to the couches and is in the process of pouring glasses of champagne. I gesture for August to take a seat. His scent envelops me as he passes by—teakwood, orange blossom, and expensive car leather. I glance out the window at the Tesla now parked in front of our store.

"If you could pick one word to describe your dream wedding," Mom asks Kathleen, "what would it be?"

I try to listen as Mom goes through her typical opening questions. I'm vaguely aware of the bride choosing the word *elegant*. I think she also tells Mom that they expect five hundred guests, many of them government officials and even minor celebrities, but my focus keeps drifting back to August, and I feel like I'm only catching every third word.

We've had our fair share of fathers and brothers that have been dragged to wedding-planning meetings in the past, and every single one of them tuned everything out by this point, choosing to fiddle with their phones (as Kathleen's father is currently doing) or listen to music through tiny white earbuds instead, or even just crossing their arms over their chests and closing their eyes, as if taking a nap in the middle of a conversation is totally appropriate behavior. It's rude and it always stings a little, but the mothers of the brides usually shrug off their behavior, like, *What can you expect from a man?*

The first time it happened, I made the mistake of explaining how, once upon a time, there were these concepts called *chivalry* and *common decency*, concepts no teenage boy—or grown man, for that matter—in our current world seemed to possess any knowledge about.

We lost the client, and Mom reminded that in our line of work, the customer is always right, even when they're rude or—worse—demeaning. Ever since then, it's been my goal to make Riddle Wedding Planning such a prestigious business that we'll be able to turn away people like that without even batting an eye.

But August isn't doing any of those things. He's leaning forward as if he's actually interested in what Mom is saying. His eyes turn glassy when Kathleen describes wanting to look like a "sexy-but-demure princess" on her wedding day, like he's trying to mentally erase the words that just came out of his sister's mouth, but other than that, he's all in. Kathleen also mentions wanting to feel regal and sophisticated, but her fiancé's a country boy who loves a down-to-earth girl, so she's considering wearing cowboy boots underneath her dress.

"Think Kate Middleton meets Daisy Duke," she tells Mom, totally serious.

August hides his smile behind his hand, meeting my gaze with twinkling eyes. He also keeps glaring at his father every time he takes out his phone, which makes my heart trip all over itself.

Finally, Mom asks the most important question she'll ask before revealing her vision boards.

"And what is your budget for the wedding?"

This is it—the moment when we find out just how big this commission might be, which in turn will tell us just how big of a break this could be for the business. I hold my breath, waiting for her answer.

Kathleen smiles. "We're going to try to keep it around one million, but Daddy doesn't mind if we go a little over.

Do you, Daddy?"

"Not at all, sugarplum," he replies, still staring at his phone.

If this number fazes Mom at all, she doesn't show it. I, on the other hand, nearly cough up a lung. I blame it on allergies and excuse myself to get a glass of water, but not before I catch August smirking at me, his lips shut in a tight line and his shoulders shaking slightly as if he's trying not to laugh.

2

***

I FaceTime Evelyn and Savannah after devouring the pizza Mom and I picked up on our way home.

True to form, Evelyn answers on the first ring (she's one of those people who is so on top of the ball that it makes other people exhausted just being around her). She's sitting at her desk in her Harvard dorm room, textbook and laptop open in front of her, with her boyfriend, Beckett, a violin virtuoso attending the Boston Conservatory of Music, draped languidly in the chair behind her, reading a slim, bent paperback and looking like the definition of an artist deep in thought. At least that's what he resembles until he hears Evelyn say, "Isla!" and then he glances over with a wide, crooked smile that would make any girl's heart melt.

Savannah, also true to form, answers on the last ring. I've only seen her dorm room—which she shares with two other girls—once, the day she moved in and gave us a virtual tour. Ever since then, I've caught her in Williamsburg coffee shops, in the main library at William & Mary, and doing her homework on a picnic blanket on one of the many grassy spaces in Colonial Williamsburg, but never in her room. A single child just like me and Evelyn, Savannah gets frustrated by the constant chatter of her roommates. I'm pretty sure she only goes there to shower and sleep.

This time is no different. She's sitting in the corner booth of her favorite sandwich shop right on the edge of campus, earbuds in, an array of books open in front of her.

"Hey," she says. "What's up?"

"I think I'm in love," I tell them.

Savannah rolls her eyes, but I don't take offense to it. This isn't the first time I've made such a declaration, although it is the first time it's been so strongly directed toward someone who isn't a movie star (hello, Timothée Chalamet) or a fictional character (looking at you, Dread Pirate Roberts).

"What's his name?" Evelyn asks, sounding genuinely interested and supportive. Beckett squats down beside her chair and drapes his arm around her shoulders. She leans back against him as he kisses her temple, and I try my best not to sigh. Not because I want Beckett but because I just want *that*. Someone to adore me like Beckett adores Evelyn. Like all of the great, brooding romantic heroes adore the women who capture their hearts.

"August Harker," I tell them.

"Mm-hmm," Savannah murmurs, distractedly writing something down in her notebook. "And how much Instagram stalking have you done?"

"Enough to know he goes to Cheever Preparatory Academy, runs cross-country in the fall and plays lacrosse in the spring, captains their championship debate team, and"—I wince—"has a gorgeous girlfriend."

"Cheever?" Evelyn asks. "Where's that?"

"Richmond," I reply.

Savannah arches a brow. "So he lives an hour away *and* has a girlfriend?"

I throw myself back on my bed, a pathetic half cry, half groan escaping my lips. "Yes, which is why I'm so miserable about it."

"How did you even meet him?" Evelyn asks. "Tourist?"

I shake my head. "Remember that big meeting Mom had today? With Kathleen Harker?"

Her eyes widen. "*Oh.*"

"August is her brother."

"How'd that go?" Savannah asks. "The meeting?"

"Okay, I think."

After Kathleen revealed her wedding budget, Mom launched into her presentation, beginning with her vision boards and then moving into the staging room. Kathleen seemed to respond well to the gold, pink, pearl, and ivory color palette Mom had selected for one of the mock reception tables. Atticus even got off his phone long enough to take Mom aside and ask how her rates compared with other wedding planners in the area.

The only snag occurred when Mom said, "We also have an elegant lavender palette which can be really beautiful for a spring wedding—"

Kathleen sucked in a breath. "Oh my word, I forgot to tell you! We had to change the date. The wedding won't be in April anymore."

Mom smiled. "Not a problem. When's the new date?"

"Well, a position has opened up on the board of my father's London firm, you see—"

"That's why we've decided to plan the wedding as a family," her mother cut in, "so we can all be together before she moves."

"—but the problem is, they need me there by the first of the year," said Kathleen. "So, we've changed the date to December ninth instead."

Mom blinked. "That's only six and a half weeks away."

Kathleen's brow furrowed. "Is that a problem? All of the other wedding planners we've met with said it couldn't be done, but if it's an issue of money, we can certainly—"

"No," Mom told her. "It's not a problem."

Kathleen exhaled and wiped a hand across her brow like she'd just dodged a bullet, while Mom looked like the person who'd been standing behind Kathleen when she dodged.

"So, let me guess," Savannah says now between sips of iced tea, "August Harker walked into your mom's office, and it was love at first sight."

Yeah, I'm *so* not falling into that trap. Savannah doesn't believe in love at first sight. She says it's just hormones and pheromones and probably some other kinds of *-mones* I know nothing about. According to her, what we think is love at first sight is really just a primal instinct to spread our genetic material and increase the general population.

"Not love at first sight," I say, even though I haven't been able to stop thinking about August all night. "But I'm definitely interested."

It must be the right answer because Savannah's tone is less suspicious as she flips through her phone to pull up his page. "He's in the National Honor Society too." Savannah squints at the screen. "And kind of gawky."

I frown. "He isn't gawky. He's tall."

"He looks like someone put him on a taffy puller and stretched him out."

Beckett whispers something into Evelyn's ear. She immediately sits up and starts typing on her laptop. Beckett stands, placing his right hand against her desk and leaning forward to stare at her monitor.

"Oh, he's cute," Evelyn says. "Totally your type."

Beckett must be extremely secure in their relationship

because he doesn't even flinch when Evelyn calls another guy cute. Instead, he motions for her to scroll down, then narrows his eyes at something.

"I don't think the girlfriend's a problem," he says.

I bolt upright. "What do you mean?"

"All of their pictures are posed." Beckett shakes his head. "She centers herself, and he's always off to the side, looking like he'd rather be anywhere else."

I swipe away the FaceTime screen and pull up August's page again. The first time I looked at August's girlfriend, all I saw was thick, glossy brown hair (expertly highlighted); perfect, straight teeth; and a body a supermodel would kill for. The type of girl whose every picture screams: *I would never spill a bowl of cereal all over my shirt, and I would die before I drove a car named Bertha.* Her arms are draped around August in every picture, and she looks so deliriously happy that when I first saw them, I assumed August was happy too. But Beckett's right—August looks stiff. Sometimes bored. Sometimes vaguely annoyed, like he's trying to control how he really feels about taking yet *another* picture.

"So, you think I have a shot?" I ask and then immediately feel like the worst sort of person because while August may not look like he's totally enraptured by his girlfriend, *she* looks like she'd be completely devastated if August broke up with her.

Beckett shrugs again. "Hard to tell from just a picture, but...yeah. I'd say so."

"Except for the fact that he lives an hour away," Savannah reminds me as she checks something in her textbook.

"And the fact that I probably won't ever see him again," I add.

"You don't think your mom will get the job?" Evelyn asks.

"We're competing against a lot of big names. It'd be like a community college trying to recruit someone who's already been accepted to the Ivy League." I let my head fall into my hands. "We don't have a chance."

"Okay, first thing: Riddle Wedding Planning is no community college. Your mom's already been featured in that magazine—what was it called?" Savannah asks.

"*Southern Fried Weddings.*"

It hadn't been a big article or anything, just a one-sentence mention with a picture of a reception area Mom had set up for our first destination wedding, with lanterns hanging from trees and old-fashioned string lights overhead, but it had included a caption that read: *Photo courtesy of Riddle Wedding Planning,* and we received eight new clients off of that picture alone.

"Yeah, that one," Savannah says. "And Kathleen Harker obviously came to you for a reason. I'd say you're on an even playing field with everyone else."

I bark out a laugh. "Yeah. Okay."

There's a knock on my door. I twist around to see Mom pushing it open, her face white.

"Mom? What's wrong?"

She doesn't speak, just moves into the room and plops onto my desk chair, staring off into space.

"Guys, I've gotta call you back." I hang up the phone before they can respond and sit up on the edge of my bed. "Mom?"

"We got it," she mumbles at the ballet flats all piled on top of one another on the floor of my closet.

"What?"

"We got it," she says again, louder this time. "Kathleen Harker just called. She said she loved our ideas and that we were the only ones who were confident we could pull off a wedding for five hundred guests in six and a half weeks."

"*What?* Mom! That's amazing. I knew you could do it!" I jump up and do a little twirl, bouncing on the balls of my feet, but Mom doesn't move. "Why aren't you excited?"

She flicks her gaze to me. "We can't pull off a wedding in six weeks."

"Of course, we can."

"For five hundred people?"

"I'm not saying it's going to be easy—"

"It's going to be impossible!" Mom drops her face into her hands. "Why did I tell her it wouldn't be a problem? *Of course, it's a problem.*"

"Mom." I peel her hands off her face and force her to look at me. "It's not a problem. We can do this. You have me, and you have Daphne. Between the three of us, we can handle it."

"But—"

"No 'buts'. We can do this. I'll work in the office every day after school, and we can work late every night. And yeah, all of our Saturdays are booked with other weddings between now and then, but Daphne can take the lead on those while we work on the Harker wedding."

Silence.

"Mom."

She looks up at me.

"We can do this," I tell her.

She closes her eyes and takes a deep breath. The color is only just beginning to return to her cheeks as she opens her eyes again and asks, "You really think so?"

My heart thumps like a caged animal against my chest. I pray she can't hear it. "I know so."

Mom laughs.

A beat passes.

Then:

"Okay."

"Okay?" I ask.

She grins. "We're going to plan a million-dollar wedding."

"Yes, we are!"

Mom jumps up and down with me, making an "Ahhhh" noise that's equal parts excitement and total fear, then she stops and begins ticking items off on her fingers while she talks. "Okay, Kathleen's meeting with us again on Saturday to look at Christmas palettes, so we'll need to go over those tonight and then write out a list of everything that needs to get done, ordering them from highest priority to lowest." She starts for the door, then stops and turns back to me. "How much homework do you have?"

A lot.

"Some."

Mom nods. "Get that done first, then meet me at the kitchen table. We've got a lot of work to do."

3

When Kathleen and her mother arrive at the office on Saturday, August isn't with them. I want to ask them where he is, but if I do that, I might as well stick a Post-It note that reads *I <3 August Harker* directly onto my forehead.

"Is your husband parking the car?" Mom asks.

Maureen shakes her head. "Atticus won't be joining us today. He's"—she lowers her voice like she's about to share top-secret information—"working on a big case, you know."

"And August?" Mom asks.

My foot catches on the corner of the rug.

"He had a sunrise practice this morning, but he should be here shortly," Maureen answers.

"Would you like to wait for him to get started?" I give Mom credit—she doesn't even glance at the clock, even though the Sommers-Powell wedding is set to begin in just four hours.

Mom didn't always want to be a wedding planner. Until

five years ago, she was content with the smaller side income she was making with the dress shop, back when her customer base was tiny but loyal, with the bulk of her profits coming from the homecoming dresses she'd get in every fall and the prom dresses every spring. But then Dad left—moved across the country with his twenty-year-old girlfriend/secretary with plans to become a big-time Hollywood agent (he's still working on it)—and Mom's entire world fell apart.

She spent days in bed. I brought her tissues and chocolate chip cookies and celebrity gossip magazines, but the one thing I didn't know how to do was make her my mom again. The mom who woke up with a smile on her face every morning. Who danced to nineties music in the kitchen while making pancakes. Who had such a joy for life that customers bought dresses from her simply because of how special she made them feel when they were in them.

I think that's why Dad's betrayal stung all the more deeply—both because he stole the light from her eyes, and because I really thought divorce was something that happened to other parents.

Mom and Dad had seemed so in love. He always knew how to make her laugh, and she always knew how to smooth his ruffled feathers. And sometimes, when she was making a pot of tea, or doing the dishes, or helping me with my homework, he would wrap his arms around her and hold her for no reason at all.

Before I fell in love with the way fictional romantic heroes gazed at the women who'd stolen their tortured hearts, I fell in love with the way my dad gazed at my mom. Like there was no one in the whole world he'd rather be with than her.

Evelyn and Savannah were both there for me when Dad left, and even though Savannah has a tendency toward brutal honesty, she didn't rattle off divorce statistics or tell me yet again that true love is a fallacy and the concept of soul mates and destiny and all of that other "fairy tale crap" doesn't hold up scientifically—she just sat with me. Cried with me. Watched my favorite romantic comedies with me (*Pretty Woman, Roman Holiday, 10 Things I Hate About You, You've Got Mail, Father of the Bride,* and *It Happened One Night*). It was in watching those movies that I became resolved to find the real thing for myself. The Happily Ever After. The marriage that wouldn't end in divorce.

Mom came back to me slowly. Ten crumpled tissues on the bed, when the day before it'd been fifteen. A cracked magazine spine. A mug of coffee she must have gotten for herself while I was at school. Then, finally, I found her sitting at the kitchen table, writing out a list of things that needed to get done on a yellow legal pad. At the top, circled three times, were the words *Find a job.*

She tried to hide the list from me.

"I'm not a little kid anymore," I told her. "I can help."

When that didn't work, I tried, "Don't lie to me like Dad did," but that just made her cry again.

Finally, on a Saturday morning, over a plate of waffles I'd made as a peace offering, I said, "We're in this together. Don't shut me out."

Finally, she told me the truth.

"Your father offered to pay this month's bills," she'd said, "but if I don't find a job soon, we're going to have to sell the house."

I took her hand in mine and held her gaze. "What can I do to help?"

Together, we typed up her resume. Searched for jobs online. Tried to figure out if we'd be better off keeping the dress shop as a side hustle or selling it.

Mom's first wedding-planning job was supposed to be a one-off, a favor for a friend who couldn't afford a "real" wedding planner. Mom didn't make a lot of money—just enough to pay for groceries for a few weeks—but she did impress another bride at the wedding, who hired Mom on the spot for her own wedding. Slowly, the business grew, and Mom realized she actually enjoyed the planning process. I helped Mom in whatever way I could, and we built the business into what it is today. It's just as much my baby as it is hers.

I'm desperate for Kathleen's wedding to go off without a hitch.

Mom asks me to wait in the lobby for August while she takes Kathleen and her mom back to the staging area. We've set up three different tablescapes for them to view—my favorite is the one with the pine-green tablecloth and matching Christmas tartan napkins; pewter chargers and silverware; and dark crimson rose centerpieces with holly, ivy, winter branches, and blood-red berries spilling out of them.

My phone rings.

Daphne.

"How's it going over there?" I whisper.

"Only half of the reception favors have been delivered, a bridesmaid decided to go on a diet for the wedding and now her dress is two sizes too big, and I spilled coffee all over my skirt."

I bite my thumbnail, thinking. "Okay, I'll pick up a bag of mini-Hershey bars and we'll stuff those in the rest of the reception bags. No one will notice they aren't the same if we keep them separated by tables, and even if they do, no one's going to complain about a chocolate bar. Safety pin the bridesmaid's dress in the back and cover the evidence with a shawl. And if you don't have an extra outfit in your car like Mom always says you should, she's going to kill you."

Daphne sighs. "Just get your mom over here as soon as possible."

"On it."

I hit End on the cell and click the screen off just as a Mercedes convertible pulls up to the curb. Through the window I watch August hop out of the car, looking adorable in a white T-shirt and gray sweatpants. He reaches into the back seat to grab an athletic bag, then turns and starts for our front door. But then the girl sitting behind the steering wheel—the girl I instantly recognize from her page as Sophie Calloway, August's girlfriend and budding social media influencer—must say something to him because he turns back.

She crooks a finger at him, a coy smile on her lips. He leans over the door and gives her a quick peck on the cheek. He starts to pull away, but she wraps her fingers around his neck, angling his head for a deeper kiss, and then she's practically chewing off the bottom half of his face, and I'm seriously considering calling someone for help before she pulls a praying mantis and bites his head off.

Finally—*finally*—she lets him go, slides on a pair of sunglasses, and takes off, almost side-swiping a minivan as she pulls into traffic.

August wipes the back of his hand across his mouth and shakes his head at her, mumbling something under his breath as he turns to head inside. The bell tinkles over the door as he walks in. Too late, I realize I should have made it look like I was busy doing something else—not just standing here, watching him like a creepy stalker this entire time.

"Sorry about that," he says, and I'm not sure if he means he's sorry he's late (because he glances at the clock) or sorry for the public display of too-much affection (because his hand does a sort of flick toward the window).

I wave off his comment. "That's okay. Happens all the time."

His brow arches.

"I mean, brides have been late to their own weddings

before, so that's nothing new." A tiny voice in my brain says, *Okay, that's fine, that's a good place to stop. Just act like that's all he meant.* "And we *are* a wedding planning company," I continue anyway, the words somersaulting out of my mouth. "We've seen our fair share of make-out sessions."

He sputters. "Oh, um...yeah. That was—"

"It's okay." *Stop talking. Stop talking NOW.* "You don't have to explain it to me. You're in love."

Are you in love?

I scan his features, trying to gauge his reaction.

He glances around the room, betraying nothing. "So... where is everyone?"

Yes, good idea. I need to surround myself with other people before I say something even more embarrassing. "In the back. Come on, I'll take you."

"Um, what should I do with...?" He gestures at his athletic bag.

"You can just set it by the door. We don't have any other appointments today."

He still takes care to drop the bag behind Daphne's reception desk so that it's out of sight. He turns back to me, giving me a lopsided grin that makes my knees go weak. "A sweaty gym bag doesn't exactly scream 'dream wedding', does it?"

I go for nonchalance, shrugging and forcing my voice to sound like a normal person's should, even though everything inside of me is melting into a puddle on the floor and I'm kind of shocked I have enough solid matter left inside of me to stand upright. "Depends on what your dream is."

He laughs at my joke, like it was something really witty to say, and I know I should act like I really *am* that clever, but it's like my brain has shut off and my mouth's on autopilot.

"No, really," I tell him. "We had this super athletic couple last year who wanted to get married at Exercise Palace in the racquetball court where they met, but the bride's parents would only pay for a traditional ceremony."

"Oh."

"Yeah."

He glances down at his shoes, his hands in his pockets.

Meanwhile, I'm trying to figure out how much it would cost to move to Alaska and change my name to something really common so no one could trace it.

"Well, for what it's worth," he says, glancing up at me from beneath his lashes, "I bet you would've thrown an incredible racquetball wedding."

"Th-thanks." I clear my throat. "I think we would have too."

I assume he's going to leave it there, that he's just being nice, but then his eyes light up, changing from the color of an incoming storm to a shining steel-gray that reminds me of skyscrapers and light bouncing off aluminum foil.

"Tell me," he says as we turn and start toward the staging room, walking slow, as if he wants to stretch out our conversation as long as possible, "would people have been actively playing racquetball during the wedding?"

"Not during the ceremony," I say, "or during dinner. We didn't think anyone needed to get a concussion halfway through the halibut course."

"You've got to admit it would've been pretty exciting though. Everyone could have kept a fork in one hand and a racquet in the other, and they could have shouted 'Jolly good shot' at each other between bites."

"'Jolly good shot'? Where were we hosting this wedding, England?"

"People say 'Jolly good shot' in America too, you know."

"In a Fitzgerald novel, maybe, but not in real life."

He walks with his hands behind his back. "Is present company to be excluded, then?"

I roll my eyes. "Please. You do not say, 'Jolly good shot.'"

"Every chance I get, old sport," he says, mimicking Leonardo DiCaprio's portrayal of Jay Gatsby perfectly, even down to the mannerisms. "Every chance I get."

A rush of breath escapes my lips. My mind is simultaneously screaming, *Where did you come from?* and *You can't be real,* because what typical teenage boy talks like this? All of the ones I've met only seem to have video games and Cool Ranch Doritos on the brain.

He laughs. "Don't get me wrong, I eat my fair share of Cool Ranch Doritos too."

Oh no. *Oh no, oh no, oh no*—

Did I really just say that out loud?

I let out a strange, squeaking, nervous chortle I've never heard in my entire life, my brain screaming at me: *FOR THE LOVE OF ALL THAT IS HOLY, KEEP YOUR MOUTH SHUT* as I reach for the door handle.

"Oh, here," he says, reaching for the handle at the same time. "Let me get that."

Our palms brush. An arc of blue lightning zaps our fingertips.

"Ouch." I pull my hand back.

August stares down at his fingers, amazed. "Wow. Literal sparks. I thought that sort of thing only happened in movies."

I laugh again as I open the door—a shaky but still more normal sound than whatever came out of my mouth a second ago. "After you."

He's still staring at his hand as he walks in. I lick my suddenly dry lips and rub my palms together, but my hand still feels just tingly as it did when August's skin brushed my own.

I take it as a good sign that Mom, Kathleen, and Mrs. Harker are sitting at my favorite tablescape. Mom has already pulled out the wedding binders we made for them this morning. They only have a couple of pages in them right now, but they'll grow as we make more decisions. I've been telling Mom we should develop an app for this, but she's old school. Maybe that's something I can focus on a couple years from now, when our business will—hopefully—have the money to spare on it.

I can see from here that Mom has Kathleen and Maureen turned to the first page, entitled *Top Priorities,* so I haven't missed much.

They're discussing possible venue sites, which means they've already gone over the top two items on the list—*Save the Date Cards* and *The Dress.* The former absolutely has to get out this coming week so people can clear their schedules. The latter also must be figured out this coming week because most dresses take six months to come in after they're ordered. Kathleen's budget will help speed up the process, but six weeks is still cutting it almost impossibly close. Mom has already set up an appointment for Kathleen with her favorite designer, Rachel Lindberg, in New York City. She and her mom will fly in tomorrow morning on their family's private airplane.

Yep. That's what I said. *Private. Airplane.*

August takes a seat next to his mother, his elbows on the armrests and his hands clasped over his stomach.

"Can I get anyone something to drink?" I offer, trying not to notice the way his white T-shirt stretches across his abs.

"I'll take a green tea," Kathleen says.

"Oh, that sounds good. Green tea for me too, please," says her mother.

Mom asks for an espresso.

At first, August says he doesn't need anything, but then, as I turn toward the door, Mom starts talking about bouquets and flower arrangements for the church, and August suddenly shoots up like his chair's on fire. "On second thought, I'll grab a water."

"Oh, there's no need for you to get up," I say, waving him back down. "I can get it for you—"

"Nonsense, you'll have your hands full," he says, widening his eyes in a *let me do this* sort of way. "Besides, I already have a water bottle in my bag."

"I could grab it for you," I say, getting a weird pleasure out of watching him squirm.

"I wouldn't dream of it," he replies, moving past me and out into the hallway. "That bag is filthy."

I follow him out of the staging room and close the French doors behind me. "Not a big fan of wedding planning?"

He follows me into the kitchenette off the back door, his cheeks turning a bright shade of pink. "I've never been into planning big events. That's my mom and Kathleen's thing."

"You could've fooled me. You seemed really interested in it the last time you were here."

The color in his cheeks deepens. "I just think if someone is talking, they deserve my full attention. But if I have the choice between going over flower arrangements and grabbing refreshments, I'll refresh people every time."

"So, you don't like big parties, then?"

He shrugs. "I like to eat the food."

I arch a brow. "A boy who's hungry all the time? Could you be more of a stereotype?"

"I also love sports movies and sleeping in."

He leans forward conspiratorially, waiting for me to match his banter with something equally clever. I try—I really do—but my mouth drops at how beautiful he looks when he smiles like that, expectantly waiting for something spectacular, and my brain shuts off instantly because I am *not* something spectacular. At least not as spectacular as his social-media-famous girlfriend (one hundred thousand followers and counting).

So instead, I blurt out the first thing that comes to mind. "Rom-coms."

He blinks. "What?"

I clear my throat. "Um, romantic comedies? Those are the movies I love."

Seriously? Could I *be* any more awkward? The only thing that would have been worse is if it had come out in Yoda-speak: *Love romantic comedies I do.*

August sticks his hands in his pockets in this super adorable way and instantly looks like a haute couture sweatpants model. "All-time favorite?"

I scoff. "That's easy. *You've Got Mail.*"

His mouth twitches in the facial-equivalent of a shrug.

My heart sinks. "Don't tell me you're one of those guys who thinks romantic comedies are ridiculous."

"Not at all," he says. "I'm just more of a Nancy Meyers fan myself. *Something's Gotta Give* is a classic. I watch it every time it's on."

Now it's my turn to blink. "Huh?"

"Don't get me wrong—I enjoy Nora Ephron as well. I mean, how can you not? She's romantic-comedy royalty, but...I don't know. I just find Nancy Meyers more uplifting, I guess."

"Wait, let me get this straight. You not only *don't* think romantic comedies are ridiculous, but you also know two of the biggest names in the entire romantic-comedy business?"

His brow arches. "Now who's stereotyping?"

"I'm sorry, I just—I didn't know that was a thing for someone...well, I mean, someone with a..." I angle my head toward the window, my own cheeks warming as I mentally relive August's face getting vacuumed off by Sophie's lips.

August barks out a laugh. "Someone with a girlfriend, you mean?"

"Exactly."

He rubs his hand across his face, his smile wide, his eyes gleaming. "My sister is a big fan. And since she's five years older than me, there was a good stretch of time there where I didn't have the strength to fight her for the remote." He shrugs. "Romantic comedies grew on me. I mean, some of them are complete garbage, but the classics? Cinematic gold."

I shake my head at him. "Could you be any more perfect?"

He frowns. "Excuse me?"

DID I JUST SAY THAT OUT LOUD?

YES. YES, I DID.

Play it off.

Play it off, play it off, play it—

"Uh, could *they* be any more perfect?" I ask. "Classic rom-coms?"

The confusion clouding his eyes disappears. His smile returns, and my heart kicks back into regular rhythm. "No, I really don't think they could."

What the hell is wrong with me? Why is every single thought that crosses my brain coming out of my mouth?

I cringe and hope he doesn't notice as I open one of the upper cabinets and grab the teacups before putting on the electric kettle for the Harkers and the espresso machine for Mom.

August leans against the counter next to me. "So, what's your deal?"

His shoulder brushes mine, and I almost drop the entire box of tea.

"What do you mean?" I ask, fumbling the teabags into their cups.

"Do you actually like wedding planning, or are you here against your will?"

"No, I really, *really* love it."

"Well, if you could find a way to inject me with some of your enthusiasm over the next six weeks, I'd appreciate it."

"Please. Six weeks is nothing. Most families have to maintain their enthusiasm for an entire year."

"Ha, yeah," he says, scratching the back of his head. "I guess rushed weddings have their perks." He gazes around the room as the water begins to boil. "Who's the Francophile?"

"Huh?"

He gestures at the picture of the Eiffel Tower over the sink.

"Oh. My mom." I pull the kettle from the warmer and pour the water into the cups, matcha powder blooming to the surface in dusty green clouds. "It's always been her dream to go. My dad promised he would take her someday, but..."

August's face is a giant question mark, but he doesn't pry, which makes me feel more comfortable telling him.

"They divorced," I explain. "A couple years ago."

He scoots closer, and I breathe him in, all teakwood and orange blossoms and the slightest hint of sweat from practice. "I'm sorry."

"Thanks." I swallow. "Now her dream is to plan a destination wedding there. Something big and grand and incredible."

"I could try to convince Kathleen to switch locations, if you'd like?"

My stomach drops. "Please don't. Planning a wedding for five hundred people in six weeks in a *foreign country*? You might as well buy a burial plot for my mom while you're at it because there's no way she would survive that."

"A bit tricky, huh?"

"A bit," I say, laughing. And then words decide to tumble out of my mouth again. "Maybe for your wedding?"

His brow arches.

"In the future, I mean. *Far* into the future. When you're

ready to settle down with"—I gesture at the window
again—"or, you know, whoever."

Stop talking.

I bite the inside of my cheeks.

August stares deep into my eyes and, completely serious, with no hint of teasing at all, says, "You'll be the
first one I call."

And if I hadn't already been half in love with him this
morning, those words and finding out that he's a Nancy
Meyers fan seals the deal.

But I'm not stupid. I know this isn't a movie. He lives an
hour away, and he comes from an entirely different world.
A world where girls like Sophie Calloway hang on his every
word and he and his family fly around in private jets whenever they want. Which means August Harker is not destined
to be my One True Love.

If anything, he's destined to be the boy who breaks
my heart.

4

***

Mom has moved on to discussing bridesmaid dresses and tuxes by the time we return. Kathleen is telling her there will be four bridesmaids and four groomsmen, plus a flower girl and a ring bearer. I lay down the teacups gently in front of Mrs. Harker and Kathleen, then hand Mom her espresso as I take the seat next to her. I open my binder and make a note to buy special baskets for both the flower girl and the ring bearer with snacks, coloring books, and other activities inside to keep them happy and busy during the wedding.

August takes the chair across from me, slouching back in a relaxed pose, his half-empty water bottle held loosely in his hand.

I try to focus on my note taking, but it's impossible to ignore him. He's just so beautiful, sitting there with his golden skin and hair the color of sand, as if he were chiseled out of sea-swept dunes. I glance up at him once. Twice. Three times.

The fourth time my gaze flicks up, my breath catches in my throat.

He's staring right back at me.

My cheeks flame as I move my gaze around the room.

Out of the corner of my eye, I see the side of his mouth twitch up.

The meeting drags on for another ninety minutes. Mom covers every detail from DJ vs. band (Kathleen picks a jazz band that is excellent but so expensive that Mom and I have never used them before), cake design, church venue and reception location (Holy Family Church in Richmond, with reception to follow in the ballroom of their country club), and décor. Even though I tell myself not to, I keep glancing at August, praying he'll do *something* to make me dislike him, but even though he's more relaxed than yesterday without his dad here, he pays just as much attention to everything Mom is saying as he did before. He even interjects with opinions on the orchestral music for the church, recommending Pachelbel's Canon for the bridal party's entrance over his sister's choice of Vivaldi's "Winter" because (and I quote), "Vivaldi is too frenetic. It makes people anxious. Play it when everyone's leaving so they'll get out faster."

I agree with August. I'm also shocked he knows who Pachelbel and Vivaldi—common wedding staples—are, but then I remember: *he's a rich kid*. He probably grew up listening to them while painting replicas of the Sistine Chapel in preschool and studying comparative philosophy in kindergarten.

It turns out Kathleen is just as easily charmed by her brother as every other girl with a heartbeat. She chooses Pachelbel.

We finally finish up with just under an hour to spare before the Sommers-Powell wedding begins. Thankfully it's only a five-minute drive to our local episcopal church.

Maureen and Kathleen slowly pack up their binders while August crinkles his empty water bottle in his hands. Mom, to her credit, doesn't check the time on her phone, nor does she look like she's running through a mental checklist of what still needs to be done for today's wedding, even though I'm sure that's exactly what she's doing.

Once everyone is ready, Mom leads the way to the door. I hang back, checking everyone's seats to make sure no purses or cell phones were left behind.

August waits for me by the French doors. For a second, I think he may have even been checking me out because he quickly looks at a spot on the wall when I turn around, his Adam's apple rolling down his throat. But I must be wrong. He has a girlfriend—a drop-dead gorgeous one at that. Why would he be looking at me?

"You didn't have to do that," I tell him, gesturing to the door he's keeping propped open with his shoulder.

"I was taught it's polite. Is that wrong? Have I made a terrible faux pas?"

He uses words like *faux pas*. I don't think half of the boys at my school even know what *faux pas* means.

"Only if you point out how polite it is," I say, shocked at my ability to form coherent—even semi-flirty—words. "Then it makes you seem like you're fishing for compliments."

"Well, we can't have that. I only fish for trout. And—on the rare occasion—bass," he says. "Although I must say, it was *incredibly* polite of me, wasn't it?"

I laugh. "You really are the last true gentleman."

His smile grows, and my heart turns into a puddle of goo sliding down my ribcage.

Why does he have to have a girlfriend?

August follows me into the main room, where Mom, Mrs. Harker, and Kathleen are waiting by the front doors. Mom reminds Kathleen of her appointment tomorrow at

Rachel Lindberg's atelier.

"Wait, you aren't coming?" Kathleen asks suddenly.

Mom's eyes widen. "It's typically a family affair—"

Kathleen grabs Mom's arm. "You *have* to be there. I'll end up falling in love with everything regardless of whether it goes with our theme or not. I need your critical eye. Both of yours," she adds, including me. "Please, say you'll come."

I look at August.

He stares back at me, a mixture of curiosity and what looks like hope in his eyes. Or maybe I'm just reading into them what I want to see.

"Of course," Mom says, patting Kathleen's hand. "We'd be delighted."

She exhales. "Oh, thank God."

August crinkles his water bottle again.

"Will your father be attending?" Mom asks.

"No, unfortunately," Mrs. Harker answers, a slight edge to her tone. "He's still working on that case, you know."

August leans forward and whispers, "There's always a case," so only I can hear, his breath tickling my earlobe. A tingle shoots from the top of my spine all the way down to my toes.

"It'll just be the five of us," Kathleen adds.

The five of us. As in, August will be there too.

"We'll send a car to pick you up and bring you to the airport," Maureen tells Mom. "The plane will be leaving at eight, so text me your home address and I'll make sure the car arrives in time."

"Thank you," Mom says. There's a slight breathiness to her words, the only sign that she's just as bowled over by the prospect of riding in a private plane to New York City as I am.

August glances back at me one last time as they start through the doors. "See you tomorrow."

"See you," I repeat, slightly dazed at the fact that this time tomorrow, I am going to be in a city I've always wanted to visit, with the most gorgeous boy in human history keeping me company.

I don't have a single clue what I'm going to wear.

5

✷✷✷

5

***

The car—a black Bentley whose rounded edges shimmer in the glow of our porchlights—picks us up at six a.m. the next day. A gentle snow is falling as the early morning temperature hovers around the freezing mark, so I switch out my ballet flats for warmer black knee-high boots and follow Mom into the car.

Mom, who said she couldn't sleep for all of the ideas galloping through her head, made whole-grain waffles for breakfast, topped with strawberries, banana slices, and the organic maple syrup she has shipped in every few months from a farm in Vermont.

I could barely eat a single bite. Mom assumed it was airplane jitters and I didn't correct her, but inside, all I kept thinking was: *How exactly am I supposed to act like a normal human being around August Harker when half the time I just want to throw myself at him and the other half I want to hide under a rock?*

Is it possible for a boy to literally make your head spin? Because mine hasn't stopped spinning since the day we met.

After a frantic FaceTime call with Evelyn and Savannah last night and literally flinging every single article of clothing I own onto my bed, I settled on a loose-fitting black turtleneck and a houndstooth skirt that stops just below my knees and cinches in at the waist. I've also slicked my hair back in an exact replica of Audrey Hepburn's low ponytail with bangs pushed to the side, and I even lined my eyes just like her too.

"Careful," Mom said as I shrugged into a vintage 1950's wool coat I scored at the local second-hand store, left unbuttoned to show off my carefully curated outfit. "You keep dressing like that, and you'll upstage the bride."

I rolled my eyes at her, even though that *can* be a concern. It's important to look professional but not too nice, or else an overly sensitive bride can start to feel like her territory is being threatened. But this may be the only time in my life that I'm riding in a private airplane to Manhattan—escorted by the cutest boy on Earth, no less.

I *have* to look my best.

The small, private airport is over an hour away, and Mom and I spend the time leaving voice mails at all of our top vendors—cake decorator, florist, caterer, stationer, photographer, makeup artist, limo service, etc.—and sketching out designs for the church and reception aesthetic. We've settled on a lantern-and-candlelight theme for the church which will carry over into the reception. Arches of evergreen boughs artfully dotted with holly and ivy will create a tunnel running the length of the aisle for the bridal party to walk through, with lanterns placed along the floor and candelabras running the perimeter of the sanctuary. Kathleen has assured us that the church will already have a dozen Christmas trees decked in white twinkle lights behind the altar, so we don't have to worry about anything there. We're in the middle of examining the ballroom pictures we found on their country club's website to determine the best reception table layout when the car slows, and I glance up.

There's a small jet waiting on the runway in front of us, and there, standing at the top of the steps leading into the plane's cabin, is August. He's wearing a perfectly cut navy peacoat with the collars turned up around his ears and the softest-looking gray scarf I've ever seen casually looped around his neck. His pants end at his ankles in the European style, showing off expensive-looking brown leather shoes, and his hair is swept back off his face, so that the angles of his cheekbones and jaw are even more pronounced than they were before. The snow has switched to a mist that seems almost suspended in the air between us, making the orbs of light surrounding the plane appear bigger and the edges around August look all soft and ha-loed, like something from a dream.

"Just think," Mom says, leaning forward to stare at the plane through my window. "People like them fly around in these things all the time. Can you imagine?"

I shake my head. "I'm just waiting for someone to pinch me."

Mom's fingers squeeze the inside of my arm.

"Ouch!" I glare at her. "I didn't mean literally."

She winks and nudges my shoulder. "Come on. Let's go knock their socks off."

The driver opens Mom's door first, then comes around to get mine. My skirt unfolds and swishes around me as I stand. August stuffs his hands into his pockets, leaning to the side in that casual gesture that makes him instantly look like he's in the middle of a photoshoot. But it's not a conscious stance—he's not *trying* to look that cute. It's just how he looks when he's comfortable. Meanwhile, I feel so fidgety inside that I must look like one of those tiny shaking chihuahuas by comparison.

Deep breaths.

"Glad to see you found the place," he calls down to us as Mom starts up the stairs.

"Are we ready to go dress shopping?" Mom asks him.

He grins. "I was born ready."

Mom chuckles as she glides past him and into the cabin.

August's eyes lock on mine. He smiles that perfect thousand-watt smile, and my heart trips all over itself again.

Be cool.

I try for a smile that says, *Oh, I forgot you were going to be here, but it's nice to see you,* instead of one that screams, *You're perfect, and I'm half in love with you already— MARRY ME?*

I open my mouth to say what I hope is a normal hello, but then my foot slips on a melting puddle of snow and, in one fluid motion, I go from walking up the stairs to pitching forward. My arms career in front of me, and then, before I can stop myself, my face smacks right into August's chest.

"Whoa." His arms wrap around my back, steadying me. "Are you okay?"

I nod into his coat, my cheeks bursting with the heat of a billion suns. "Just embarrassed."

"Oh yes. You really should be embarrassed. After all, no one has ever slipped on a patch of snow before."

I tilt my head back just enough to glance up at him.

He grins down at me. "There she is."

My lips twitch as I stand back up.

"Is your ankle okay?" he asks. "I sprained mine on that very step a few years ago. It killed for weeks."

"Snow?"

"Rain."

"Ah, the other wet stuff."

"You know, people always rant and rave about how beautiful sunny days are, but I actually prefer rainy ones. When they aren't trying to take out my ankles, that is."

"Me too," I tell him. "There's something about dark, gray skies that makes the world feel...I don't know...smaller somehow."

"Cozier," he agrees. "Not to mention the best romantic-comedy moments happen in the rain."

I nod. "The best makeups."

"And the best breakups," he counters.

"The best kisses."

"The best proposals."

I swallow.

"Is it just me," he asks, leaning forward slightly, "or do people seem to fall in love more easily in the rain?"

I stare up into his own stormy eyes. The mist has dampened his hair, so that a few tendrils have fallen to frame his temples, small beads of water dripping from their ends. He's so beautiful—all sharp lines and kind lips and a gaze that makes you feel like you're the only person in the entire world—that all I want to do is cry.

"It's not just you," I murmur.

He smirks. "You know, I'm beginning to think I may have found a kindred spirit in you, Isla Riddle."

And that's when I realize—I'm no longer against his chest, but his arms are still wrapped around me. Much, much longer than they needed to be for me to find my footing.

August's eyes widens as he realizes this as well. He takes a hurried step back.

He clears his throat. "We, uh, better get inside before they decide to take off without us."

I expect him to be standoffish now that things have gotten so unbearably awkward, but as I step through the door, his hand appears underneath mine, steadying me.

The contact is brief—there and gone—but it sends a shiver all the way down to my toes.

Kathleen and her mom are sitting at a table next to the windows. Towering stacks of bridal magazines are strewn between them, each one sporting cracked spines and pages brimming with color-coordinated sticky notes and dogeared corners. There's also a tablet in front of them that Kathleen consults, comparing and contrasting whatever is written there with the magazine photos her mother is showing her. My mom sits on the other side of her, gently offering advice every time the other two women pause for a breath. It looks less like they're planning a wedding and more like they're planning a full-scale military operation.

Two untouched cappuccinos and a plate of avocado toast rest on the windowsill between them, completely forgotten.

Mrs. Harker glances up as August and I walk in.

"Ah, there you two are," she says. "I was wondering where you'd gotten to. We were about to leave without you."

"Told you," August whispers in my ear.

"Would you like anything to drink, Isla?" Mrs. Harker asks me. "Tea? Cappuccino?" Her brows arch. "Mimosa?"

I shake my head. "No, thank you."

I take one of the leather armchairs in the back of the cabin, ready to jump in if they need anything. August plops down into the armchair across from me. There's a Cheever Preparatory Academy satchel already next to it and an iPad charging on the little table attached to the chair. I look for a similar table on mine, but there isn't one.

August must guess what I'm thinking because he says, "It's underneath the armrest."

I lift the armrest, and out pops the same small table, just big enough for a tablet or an oversized phone. There's also a little cupholder in the corner.

"Impressive," I tell him.

He ducks his head slightly, almost like he's...embarrassed. I'm not sure why he would be, though. I'm trying to get up the nerve to ask him about it when he leans forward, elbows on his knees, and says, "I was thinking about you last night."

My heart stops.

"What?" I sputter. "I mean, huh? I mean...why?"

"There was a rom-com marathon on TV. Two Nora Ephrons followed by two Nancy Meyers, so naturally I watched them all and then compared and contrasted them. You know, to get a less biased, more logical analysis. And I have to say, I still prefer Nancy Meyers by the slimmest of margins, although Tom Hanks and Meg Ryan are pretty tough to beat. That dog in *You've Got Mail* doesn't help. Barney?"

"Brinkley," I whisper.

"Ah, yes." He smirks. "The ever-charming Brinkley."

"You watched four romantic comedies last night?"

He shrugs. "Couldn't sleep."

The way he says this makes me think insomnia may be a recurring problem for him.

"If it makes you feel any better," I reply, "you look great."

His brow arches.

OH MY STARS, DID THAT REALLY JUST COME OUT OF MY MOUTH?

I backpedal. "I mean, you don't look like you couldn't sleep. You don't have any bags under your eyes, and you look, you know, all put together nicely." *Wrap it up.* "How many hours of sleep did you get?"

"Four." He half smirks. "I credit Nancy Meyers. No one can watch one of her films and not feel cheery the next day no matter how little sleep they've gotten. I'm pretty sure it's Newton's fourth law."

"I contend that one can say the same about Nora Ephron."

"Depends on the Ephron movie in question," he retorts, his eyes sparkling. "Nancy always delivers the feel-good ending."

"So does Nora," I say, leaning forward another inch. "But she also understands that life doesn't always wrap itself up in a perfect bow."

"Ah, but isn't that the point of a good movie? To take us away from the troubles of real life?"

"Or to show us that the bittersweet things in life are just as important and beautiful as the happy things."

His brows arch. "Touché."

My cheeks warm.

The moment stretches between us like a cord, pulling tighter and tighter.

August's phone chirps.

"You won this round, Riddle." He leans back in his seat. "But don't expect it to happen again. I'm not sure if you're aware, but I'm the captain of my school's championship debate team."

I'm aware.

He glances down at his phone, and that smile that I love so much vanishes. He curses under his breath as he tosses his phone onto the table. It skids across the small wooden panel and tumbles onto the floor.

August doesn't reach for it.

I hesitate. "Everything okay?"

He grits his teeth. "It's just my—" He stops. "Sophie."

I don't know why he doesn't want to call her his girlfriend. Did they break up? *Please tell me they broke up.*

I clear my throat. "Your girlfriend?"

He nods.

My chest deflates.

"She's pissed she's not coming today," he explains. "She thinks she should be included. I told her it's family only, and now she feels like that says something about our relationship that we—that *I*—don't see her as family, even though we've only been dating for nine months." He rubs his thumb across his bottom lip. "You coming along doesn't help matters."

"Sorry," I say, even though my heart thrills at the knowledge that I'm here for a "family-only" event and his social-media-famous girlfriend isn't. Granted, I'm here in a professional capacity, but still.

He shrugs. "She's always pissed about something. If it wasn't this, it'd be something else."

Then why are you with her?

Thankfully, the words don't slip out of my mouth this time, but I make a mental note to watch what I'm thinking around him because apparently my tongue can't be trusted.

August leans forward again. "Now, where were we? Oh yes. I was about to school you in Nancy Meyers."

"I would like to take this opportunity to interject that I actually love Nancy Meyers very much."

"Oh no, it's too late for that. You've picked your side, Riddle. It's time for you to defend it."

Now it's my turn to roll my eyes, but I laugh as I do because he's looking at me like our sparring is the most fun he's had in weeks, and my chest slowly inflates again as I say, "All right. You're on."

6

***

Rachel Lindberg's atelier is located in SoHo, which August tells me is one of the most expensive places to live in New York City. Gazing up and down Mercer Street, I can see why. SoHo is exactly what comes to mind when people think of Manhattan: beautiful old buildings all squashed together on a tight, brick-paved street, with Halloween decorations of autumn wreaths and corn stalks and various-sized pumpkins sitting along stoops and framing doorways.

The atelier is located in an ivory, six-story building with decorative columns and cornices on every level and floor-to-ceiling windows reflecting the buildings across the street and the sky above. The design inside is even more luxurious, everything decorated in soft pinks and creams, with vases and bowls of pink peonies decorating nearly every surface. A round white couch sits in the center of the consultation room, where Rachel Lindberg greets us with a tray of chocolate-covered strawberries and glasses of champagne. Mom lets me sip a little before taking it back.

Rachel starts by having her sales associate bring out different gown styles for Kathleen to exclaim over: mermaid, A-line, ball gown, trumpet, and column. After being plied with a cheese-and-fruit plate, Kathleen chooses three favorites and follows Rachel into the back dressing room. There aren't any price tags on the samples, but Mom told me the cheapest gown Rachel Lindberg makes is ten thousand dollars.

I try to focus on Kathleen every time she comes out wearing a new dress (she ends up trying eight), but, just like yesterday, my eyes keep flicking back to August. He's just so fascinating to watch. He doesn't grumble or complain about spending his Sunday morning looking at wedding dresses. He doesn't sigh or roll his eyes when Kathleen says she wants to try on the first three again to compare. He doesn't start scrolling social media on his phone when Rachel goes over all of the options of the custom work they can do on Kathleen's limited timetable ("Unfortunately, we're cutting it a bit close for an entirely custom gown, but we can certainly mix and match some of your favorite pieces from each gown to create something new"). I don't think August even brought his phone with him from the plane, which blows my mind. I don't know a single kid in my high school who would willingly part with their phone, myself included. But August seems completely at ease with not being connected to anything or anyone beyond this moment.

He reminds me of the first romantic leads my mom introduced me to when I was younger: Clark Gable and Jimmy Stewart; Fred Astaire and Gene Kelly. Like he belongs to a different time entirely, a time when minutes passed more slowly and people actually did stop and engage with whatever was right in front of them instead of constantly running from one thing to another.

I think I like that about him more than anything else—the fact that he can be so present and so supportive of his sister. I do wonder, though, as Kathleen and Rachel discuss taking the trumpet style of one dress and adding the embroidered lace sleeves of another, if August is worried what Sophie will think about him not texting her back. Somehow, I don't think he really cares, and while part of me is silently squealing inside at the prospect that maybe Beckett was right—maybe August *isn't* as completely infatuated with Sophie as I thought he was—another part of me doesn't think that speaks very well to his character, that he would stay with someone he doesn't even like all that much just because...why? She's gorgeous? Rich enough to drive a Mercedes? Has a hundred thousand followers on Instagram?

That same question that floated through my mind yesterday pops into my head again as I stare at his profile, taking in the hard line of his jaw, the slash of his cheekbones, the way that stubborn lock of hair keeps falling into his eyes whenever he leans forward, laughing at something his sister said.

Why are you with her?

It's been three hours since we first arrived, and Kathleen, Mom, and Mrs. Harker are only just now starting the long process of paying for the dress and going over a fitting schedule. Meanwhile my stomach is growling and I'm starting to feel lightheaded. I really should have eaten those waffles. I cover my stomach with my arms, trying to hide it.

Of course, August notices.

"Hungry?" he asks.

I shake my head. "No."

He arches a brow.

I sigh. "Starving."

"Wait here."

He walks over and whispers something to Mrs. Harker. She darts a glance at me, then turns to my mom.

Mom looks at me and nods.

August heads back over.

"Come on," he says, taking my hand. "Let's get out of here."

I shiver at the feeling of his palm gliding against mine.

"Where are we going?" I ask. I glance back at Mom, but she's busy discussing timelines, making sure Kathleen will be able to secure two fittings before the big day.

"To the best place in the world," he tells me, and my heart picks up again because if August Harker—a boy who rides in private airplanes and drinks champagne like he was born with a bottle of Dom Perignon in his hands—is taking me to the best place in the world, I can't even begin to imagine where that must be.

✱✱✱

"A restaurant," I say, blinking up at the building in front of me. "You've brought me to a restaurant."

Unlike the atelier's ivory coloring, this building is plaster white—the white of Italian Renaissance statues and presidential busts. It's also five stories, done in a very similar architectural style as all the other buildings on Mercer Street, but the first floor, where the restaurant is held, has expanded the glass windows so that only the decorative columns break them up—otherwise, it's a panoramic view right inside the restaurant from the street.

"Not just any restaurant," August replies. "A three-Michelin-star restaurant with the most brilliant head chef you'll ever meet."

The name *aeliana* is written in gold, lower-case letters across the top.

"That's his daughter's name. Aeliana. She's in second grade, and her younger brother, Luca, is in pre-K this year."

"Are you friends with the family or something?" I ask.

"Or something." He smirks. "Come on, let's go put our names in for a table."

I check the time on my phone. It's fifteen minutes to noon, and the entryway is packed with people trying to get tables. I overhear the hostess tell the group in front of us that the wait is over an hour long. My stomach growls again. I'm about to tug on August's sleeve and politely suggest we go somewhere else, but then the group moves out of the way and the hostess lets out a high-pitched squeal.

"August!" She moves around the podium to give him the tightest hug I've ever seen, her thick, lustrously curly hair draping over his shoulder as her entire body presses up against him in a way that makes me instantly jealous, even though I'm not his girlfriend and have nothing to be jealous of.

"I want you to meet someone," August tells the hostess as she lets him go. He reaches back and grabs my hand, tugging me forward. "This is Isla Riddle. Isla, this is my cousin, Lily."

His cousin. Lily.

"Nice to meet you," she says, shaking my hand before turning back to August and ruffling his hair. "You've grown six inches since I last saw you."

"More like three," he replies.

"Why haven't you been coming by?" she asks.

"You know Dad. Big case, important clients, yada yada. And Mom's been busy with charity functions and DAR meetings. The only reason we're here today is for Kathleen's wedding dress."

"Ah," Lily says, her attention turning to me. "So, this is the new girlfriend. I have to say, I'm really glad you dropped the old one. What was her name? Polly? Tori? Dory?"

"Sophie."

"Ugh, yeah. *Her*. Talk about uptight. And possessive. And super self-centered, by the way. I'm *so* glad you dumped her."

"Um, actually"—August scratches the back of his head—"Isla works for her mom's wedding planning company. She's just a friend. I'm still with Sophie."

Lily sucks in a breath. "Crap. Forget I said anything. Sophie's nice. *Really.* When she wants to be."

"Don't worry about it," August tells her. "It's not the first time someone's called her out on those things."

Again—*why are you with her?*

"Is Caio back there?" August asks.

Lily nods. "Go on ahead. I'll get your usual table ready."

"Thanks, Lil," he says, kissing her on the cheek. "You're the best."

"Don't I know it."

And then, once again, as if it's the most natural thing in the world for him to do, August squeezes my hand and leads me through the crowd. We weave around tables and waiters and head all the way to the back of the restaurant—

Right into the kitchen.

"Augie!" A man wearing a white chef's jacket shouts as soon as he sees August.

"Cai!" August shouts back before doing that man-hug thing where they clap their hands together and then bump into each other.

"It's been a long time, man. I thought you'd gotten too high and mighty for us," the chef says.

"Never," August tells him. "What have I missed?"

"Nothing much," the head chef—Caio—answers. "Business is booming, Aeliana's on the honor roll, and Luca's obsessed with Spider-Man."

I'm starting to learn that August has many smiles. There's his mischievous smile, the one he aims at me while debating rom-com legends and taking me to unknown locations. There's his humble smile, the one that creeps along his lips and makes his head duck down and his foot do this really adorable *Aw, shucks* sort of thing (that one might actually be my favorite). There's his pleasantly surprised smile, the one that makes his eyes twinkle like a little kid's on Christmas morning. And finally, there's his genuinely happy smile, the one he gives his mom every time she pulls him in for a side hug or that he gives his sister every time she asks for his opinion.

The one he gives *me* whenever I say something that makes him laugh.

But this—the smile he gives Caio, here, in a stainless-steel kitchen ringing with the clatter of pans being shimmied on stovetops and orders being called out and knives quickly dicing through vegetables—reminds me of the sunrise. It is a bright thing, full of hope and awe and wonder.

It makes my heart ache just looking at it.

Caio's gaze slides to me. "And who is this?"

"Isla Riddle," August says, "and before you say anything else, she's just a friend."

Caio glances at him. "Can she be trusted?"

"I don't know," August answers, turning to me, his eyes twinkling. "Can you?"

"Um...yeah," I say. "I think so."

August bobs his head. "Good enough for me."

Caio moves deeper into the kitchen. August starts to follow him, but I put my hand on his arm, stopping him.

"What exactly am I being trusted with?" I whisper.

"Government secrets," he murmurs back. "If they find out you snitched, you'll be executed at dawn."

"Excuse me?"

But August is already three steps ahead of me, his shoulders shaking with barely concealed laughter.

Caio claps his hands together as we approach. "Now then, what are we trying today? Lobster? Carpaccio? I have a new truffle risotto I've been tweaking—perhaps I could get your thoughts on that?"

"Of course," August says, hands in his pockets once more, his full attention fixed on Caio.

"Who's in your party today?"

"Just Mom and Kathleen. Oh, and Isla's mom."

"They'll want scallops, then, and my world-famous arugula salad. Have you had it before?" Caio asks, and it takes me a second to realize he's looking at me.

I shake my head.

"This is Isla's first time here," August tells him.

"Ah, well then, we shall have to make something extra special for her." He winks at me before grabbing a rolled-up apron from a stack underneath one of the steel countertops and handing it to August.

August's mischievous smile returns as he loops the apron around his neck and ties it around his waist. "Promise not to tell?"

"That you're cooking our food today?" I ask.

"That I cook at all," he says, following Caio to an empty stovetop.

I stand back and watch as August moves back and forth from the ingredients Caio is setting on the counter to the stove, throwing mushrooms and wild rice into a pot, gently laying scallops onto a pan to sear, browning shallots, garlic, and rosemary in another pan before shimmying it back and forth over the flames. Caio works next to August, showing him how to make the sauce for the scallops and instructing him when to add the stock to the risotto.

I already knew August was a confident guy. It pulses off everything he does. You can even feel it in his Instagram pictures—not in the ones Sophie takes, but in the ones people tag him in, where you see that confident smirk lighting up his face while competing with his debate team, or the ones where you see his genuinely happy smile after he's crossed the finish line of a race or scored a goal in lacrosse. But there's a natural ease to his movements here, a lightness I haven't seen anywhere else. For the first time, I realize that for his many, many smiles and the many, many millions of dollars in his family's bank account, August is never care-free. He hides it well, with his casual poses and easy-going demeanor, but it's there in the way he walks with his shoulders tucked and his head slightly down, as if gravity pulls on him a little harder than the rest of us.

But here, he stands straight and tall. Here, his wrists flick pan ingredients into the air and back down again. Here, his hands chop vegetables in that way I thought only Food Network stars could do, and he moves from one dish to the next with a fluidity that is mesmerizing to watch.

Here, he is completely free.

Less than half an hour later, a platter of perfectly seared scallops in a creamy sauce sits next to a bowl holding the most decadent-looking risotto I've ever seen, with slivers of black truffle and dots of something bright green artistically applied in a circular pattern on top. A salad tossed in a light citrus oil completes the lineup.

Caio claps his hand on August's shoulder. "Thanks for the help."

"Thanks for the lesson," August replies as he unties his apron and lays it on the counter.

"Anytime, my brother, anytime," Caio says. "You better get out there though before your mom gets suspicious."

August salutes him, then turns back to me. "Ready?"

I shake my head, amazed. "So, you're a chef as well as captain of a championship debate team?"

"Did I not mention our lacrosse team won State last year too?"

"No, you didn't," I tell him as he leads me toward the

kitchen door with a gentle hand barely touching the small of my back. "And you're avoiding the question."

He scratches his forehead with his thumb. "Yeah, it's, uh... sort of a passion of mine."

"I couldn't tell."

"In all seriousness, please don't tell anyone I helped Caio today."

"Why is it such a big secret?"

We make our way into the dining room. August scans the crowd for Kathleen and our moms, but they're not here yet.

He relaxes as we head back toward the entrance, taking a seat on an empty bench. "My dad doesn't approve."

"Why not?" I ask, sitting down next to him.

He suddenly looks like the weight of the world is pulling him down again, driving him into the center of the earth. "He wants me to go to law school. Join the firm. Make partner before I'm thirty. Have my name on the building by forty. You know, continue the legacy."

"Why wait until forty?" I tease, bumping his shoulder. "Why not just do it as soon as you graduate law school?"

"He's made it clear he's not going to make it easy on me. He's going to work me harder than anyone else in the firm—can't make it look like he's playing favorites. I'll have to earn it. Give my life to the firm, like he's done."

"But that's not what you want?"

"What gave it away? The utter lack of enthusiasm in my voice? The terror in my eyes?"

"The clenching of your fists?"

He looks down at his hands. His veins are twice their normal size, and his knuckles look like razor blades. He stretches his fingers out.

"Law has just never been a passion of mine," he explains. "I'm not even sure it's Dad's. I mean, it might have started out that way, but..." He turns toward me, laying his arm across the back of the bench. "Did you know he grew up in one of the poorest neighborhoods in DC?"

I shake my head, feeling a little dizzy at the closeness of him.

"It was just him and my grandma. His dad skipped out when he was two. My parents started dating in undergrad, so Mom talks a lot about how Dad used to be. He wanted to study constitutional law and become a politician so he could help people—change the policies that make it harder for lower-income families to get the help they need to make a better life for themselves. But then a buddy of his was interning for a defense attorney and talking about how much money his boss made, the kind of house he lived in, the cars he drove. Dad saw all of those material things he'd always wanted, all the things he told himself he would someday be able to afford, and that's what got him in the end." August clenches his teeth. "And that, ladies and gentlemen, is how my dad, Atticus Harker, went from being one of the good guys to helping billionaires break the law and get away with it. But, you know, at least he's got his mansion and his private plane and his yacht to cheer him up whenever he might feel a little bit bad about it."

"You guys have a yacht too?"

His brows arch.

"Sorry," I say. "Not the point."

August stares down at his shoes. "I just don't think I could do that. Help rich people get richer, no matter who it hurts. I really think it would kill me."

"Have you told him that?"

"I've tried. He doesn't listen. He thinks growing up with money has made me soft. Says I don't know what it's like, what he's been through, and I get that—I do—but I just don't think it gives anyone the right to become a villain."

"You think your dad's a villain?"

"Don't you?"

I squirm in my seat, suddenly uncomfortable with where this conversation is heading. "I don't know him well enough to say."

"Trust me, it doesn't take long to get a good read on him."

"So, you come here to get lessons from Caio, and he and Lily keep it a secret from your family?"

He nods.

"Does anyone else know?"

"Just you."

"But"—I shake my head—"you don't even know me. For all you know, I get my jollies sharing other people's secrets."

August bursts out laughing. "*Get your jollies*? When were you born, 1958?"

I elbow him in the side. "I'm serious. The second your mom gets here, I'm fessing up to everything."

"*Fessing up!*" He laughs harder, rocking back in his seat, his hand on his chest. "You sound like a gangster in one of those cheesy mafia movies."

Warmth bubbles in my chest, and suddenly all I want to do is make him laugh until he can't breathe, until all of the pain and disappointment and uncertainty about the future leaves his eyes. Until he smiles again and really means it.

"Now listen here, Johnny," I say, using my best Chicago gangster voice. "I ain't gettin' locked up for this, understand?"

"Stop, please." August takes deep breaths, wiping his hands across his eyes. Finally, he leans his head back against the wall. "I can't remember the last time I laughed like that. You really are the best, you know that?"

I blush.

"Seriously though," I say, my voice suddenly tight. "Why me? I mean, you could've come down here by yourself. Left me back at the atelier."

"I guess you just seemed—I don't know—like you'd understand. Somehow." His eyes flick up, meeting my gaze. "And because I wanted you to know that there's more to me than the privilege I was born into."

"Why would that matter to you?"

His lips part, and I can see something forming in his eyes—an answer, or maybe another question—but then the door opens and Mrs. Harker walks in, followed by Mom and Kathleen, and the moment disappears so suddenly, I wonder if it was ever really there to begin with.

"Darling, I'm so sorry," she says, crossing to August. "We got hung up on the sleeve length—full length, three-quarters, cap. The conversation went back and forth so much, you'd think we were trying to settle the national debt crisis."

"Which one did you go with?" I ask.

"Full length," Kathleen says, beaming, "with little thumb hooks."

"It's going to be stunning," Mom says.

Mrs. Harker kisses August on the cheek. "I hope you weren't too bored waiting for us."

"Not at all," August says. "In fact, we quite enjoyed ourselves. Isla here does a marvelous mafia impression."

"That's nice, dear," Mrs. Harker says, glancing at me with a furrowed brow before sweeping her gaze over the packed restaurant.

I wait until Mrs. Harker is distracted by Lily, then kick August in the shin.

He sucks in his lips to keep from laughing. "What was that for?"

"Mafia impression? Really? As if I haven't already given your mom enough reasons to think I'm a total spaz."

"You know, you're cute when you blush."

My heart stops.

"Like a chipmunk," he continues, suddenly looking at

the floor, the ceiling, the people sitting around us—everywhere but at me. "Or a little baby bunny."

Oh.

"Gee," I say, rolling my eyes, "what a compliment."

He laughs again. Maybe I'm imagining it, but it seems more strained than before.

"Your table is ready," Lily announces. "Chef Caio went ahead and already prepared your meal for you."

"Oh, how lovely," Mrs. Harker says, following Lily to our table. The salad, scallops, and risotto already sit in the middle, ready to be served family style, along with a steaming basket of rolls fresh from the oven. Mrs. Harker glances back at August. "Did you do this, darling?"

He stumbles.

"Yes," I say, quickly. "He ordered while we were waiting."

August exhales. He waits until the others are seated and busying themselves with the silverware and napkins before leaning over and whispering, "Thank you," in my ear.

"Don't mention it," I murmur back because if I can't be the girl he dreams about every night, at least I can be the girl he trusts to keep the deepest, most secret parts of him safe. Because I'm not unrealistic. I know our relationship—if you can even call it that—has an expiration date. And if August Harker is going to walk out of my life the day after Kathleen's wedding, I would rather he do it thinking of me as a friend than as nothing at all.

7

***

"**W**ait a minute. Repeat that again, slowly. How *exactly* did he say it?" Evelyn asks. She and Beckett are sitting in a dining hall, a half-eaten brownie perched on a plate between them.

"'You're cute when you blush,'" I repeat, flinging myself back on my bed. The afternoon sunlight filters through the tree outside my window, casting gently swaying leaf shadows up my wall. "What could that possibly mean?"

Beckett shrugs. "That he thinks you're cute when you blush?"

"Yeah, but someone who has a girlfriend shouldn't say something like that, right?" I roll over onto my stomach, propping myself up on my elbows and laying my phone against the pillows. "Unless he was saying it as a friend?"

"Oh yes," Beckett replies. "I say that to my friends all the time."

I roll my eyes. "You know what I mean. He looked super uncomfortable when he realized what he said, and

then he followed it up by comparing me to small wood-
land animals."

"Probably because he's into you and feels bad he said it,"
Savannah replies from her side of the split screen.

"But if that's true—which, by the way, I *highly* doubt—
do you think it means he wants to break up with Sophie
and, I don't know...be with me?"

No one answers.

I groan. "Ugh, it sounds even more ridiculous when I
say it out loud."

"Why?" Evelyn asks.

"Because she's out there looking like the next Miss Universe, and I'm over here just trying not to spill anything
on any more of my clothes."

"Hey, that's one of my best friends you're talking about,"
Savannah says, bits of dirt crumbling from the earthen
wall surrounding her. "And she only spills things on her
clothes once or twice a month *max*."

"Where are you?" I ask.

She huffs out a breath, blowing a strand of hair out of her
eyes. "At an archaeological dig site. I need the extra credit
for my colonial history class."

"Why? I thought you were crushing that one."

"Did your dyslexia act up again?" Evelyn asks gently.

"No," Savannah says. "All my tricks are still working. It
still takes me twice as long as anyone else to read a page,
but I swear I retain it better. Half the kids in my class still
don't know the difference between the Articles of Confed-
eration and the Constitution. And...I've also been getting
some help from this guy."

I smirk. "A guy, huh?"

She rolls her eyes. "He's just a friend, Isles."

"Uh-huh," I say. "Sure, he is."

"So, if you're doing okay," Evelyn asks before Savannah

can retaliate, "why the extra credit?"

Savannah grits her teeth, annoyed. "I slept through my midterm. Set an alarm on my phone and went to sleep without realizing it wasn't on the charger. Battery died in the middle of the night."

Evelyn gasps. That's a legitimate nightmare of hers. She's told us countless times of waking up in a cold sweat because she missed a test due to a faulty alarm.

"And I can't retake it," Savannah continues, "because my professor worries about cheating, so my friend convinced him to let me do this as an alternative. He says if I stick it out for the rest of the semester and don't miss any more tests, I'll get my A." She looks around the hole she's in, roots sticking out of the dirt around her like skeletal fingers reaching for her hair.

My eyes widen as something dark scurries up the wall behind her. "Was that a spider?"

"Oh, there are plenty of spiders," Savannah tells us. "And ants. And worms. *So* many worms."

Evelyn looks like she's going to be sick, although I can't tell if it's from all of the bug talk or if she's still reeling from the thought of missing a midterm. "Can we get back to talking about Isla's boyfriend?"

I wince. "He's not my boyfriend."

"Not yet," Evelyn teases.

"Probably not ever," I tell her. "I mean, who am I kidding? Even if he broke up with his girlfriend, he lives an hour away. And his family owns a private plane *and* a yacht. Meanwhile I barely have enough money to keep Bertha alive."

Savannah huffs out a breath. "You've helped your mom go from owning a bridal store that barely made ends meet to now helping her plan a million-dollar wedding. Give yourself some credit."

"We still come from two completely different worlds."

"Maybe he doesn't care about any of that," Evelyn interjects. "After all, he did say he wanted you to know that there's more to him than his family's money."

"Yes, but why?"

"Because he thinks you're cute," Savannah replies in a matter-of-fact way as she dusts dirt from her jeans (everything regarding love is matter-of-fact for her).

"Yeah, in a friendly neighborhood chipmunk sort of way," I grumble.

"I still think he meant more than that," Evelyn replies, elbowing Beckett in the ribs for eating over half of their brownie without her.

"Did I imagine the conversation we just had regarding the use of cellular phones at my dig site, Miss Mason?" a guy's voice calls from somewhere above Savannah— half-teasing, half-serious.

Savannah glances up at him. "Oops. Gotta go. Call you guys back later."

"When you're somewhere far, far away from here," the guy tells her.

"Absolutely," she replies with a too-sweet smile, and then her side of the screen disappears.

We're all quiet for a moment.

"I have an idea," Beckett pipes up. "Why don't you just ask him?"

I grab the phone off the pillow and sit back up. "Ask him what?"

"If he thinks you're cute in a *friendly* way or in a *girl-friend-ly* way."

Evelyn and I both stare at him, horrified.

"What?" He glances back and forth between us. "What'd I say?"

I shake my head at him. "You can't be serious."

"Why not?"

"What am I supposed to do? Walk up to him and say, 'Oh, hello, I know we've only known each other for four days, but I think I've been getting signals that you might be interested in leaving your supermodel girlfriend so you can go out with me instead?' I don't think so."

"Yeah, I agree. She might come across as desperate," Evelyn says. "No offense."

"None taken," I reply because the fact that I'm going around in circles talking about a boy I just met proves how desperate I am.

Beckett leans back in his seat in that relaxed guy pose that a girl could never do while wearing a skirt. "All I'm saying is Ev and I weren't very upfront with each other about our feelings, and it almost kept us from being together. Maybe asking him outright will get the ball rolling."

"Rolling where? Embarrassment City? Mortified, USA?"

Beckett shrugs. "At least then you'd have your answer."

"I still have to see this guy who-knows-how-many times over the next six weeks, plus I need to help Mom pull off this wedding—I can't exactly do that if I want to crawl into a hole and die whenever I'm around him." I pull my knees into my chest, wrapping my free arm around my legs. "No, this mission requires subtlety. Analyzing expressions. Evaluating tones."

"Calculating whether he's genuinely flirting with you or just engaging in witty banter," Evelyn adds.

Beckett stares at us as if we're speaking a completely different language. "Is this really the stuff that goes through a girl's head when she likes a guy?"

"Not me," Evelyn says, scrunching her nose. "I mostly just thought about how much I hated you until I realized I actually loved you."

He narrows his eyes at her. "Don't do that nose-scrunching thing. You know I can't resist you when you do that nose-scrunching thing."

"What?" she asks innocently. "Like this?"

She scrunches her nose even more.

He shakes his head, smiling. "Okay, you asked for it."

And then he's kissing her all over her face and she's squealing and batting him away, and I'm just sitting there, feeling like the most useless third wheel that ever existed.

"Okay, then," I say. "I'm going to let you guys go and do... whatever it is you're doing. Thanks for kind of helping."

"Talk soon!" Evelyn giggles into the phone.

I end the call and wonder how long it'll take her to notice the rest of the brownie is missing, or how long it'll take Beckett to buy her a brand new one to make up for it.

I lie back on my bed once more and take deep, steadying breaths, but no matter how hard I try to focus on something else—*anything* else—I can't stop seeing August.

Flashes of scenes from today keep looping through my head, one right after the other: August standing at the top of the staircase leading into the airplane, looking like the prince in every fairy tale; August listening intently and offering advice as his sister agonized over her wedding dress options; August shimmying pans and stirring pots and creating a culinary symphony that made me desperate to know even more about this boy who was already becoming the object of my every waking thought; and finally, August laughing and wiping tears from his eyes while looking at me as if I might just be the best person in the entire world for making him laugh like that.

The only small measure of comfort I have is the fact that if all of this blows up in my face, at least I'll have that as a defense—because, really, a boy cannot look at a girl like that and expect her *not* to fall in love with him any more than the moon can pull at the tide and expect the water not to recede.

8

✳✳✳

Two nights later, I'm sitting on one of the staging room's dining chairs, now stationed just outside our office, handing out candy to trick-or-treaters while Mom waits for Maureen and Kathleen to arrive. From here, they'll walk to our florist and stationery store. I'd go with them, but someone needs to be here to make sure another sixth-grader dressed like a ninja doesn't steal all the candy again like last year, and Daphne can't do it because she's answering emails, organizing contracts, putting numbers into spreadsheets—all of the stuff that has to get done for our business to run but that Mom and I loathe doing with every fiber of our beings. The day we realized we were making enough money to hire an assistant who could handle those things for us was the best day of our lives. It also allows us to focus on more weddings, and since more weddings means more money, who knows? Maybe someday we'll be able to afford two assistants and then four and then twelve and then twenty—a giant office building *full* of Daphnes and other wedding planners working for us.

A wedding empire—*that's* my dream. Not for the money, even though it would be nice to not have to worry about it anymore (although hearing Atticus Harker's origin story makes me question how much money a person can make before they start to compromise everything they used to stand for) but because when two people fall in love and decide they want to spend the rest of their lives together, I want Riddle Wedding Planning to be the place that makes their dream wedding come true.

So far tonight, I've seen three Disney princesses, four superheroes, a witch, a hockey player, a fairy queen, and Rudolph the Red-Nosed Reindeer. But the thing that shocks me the most is when Maureen and Kathleen's car pulls up, and August—wearing the same sweats with his school emblem on them that he wore the other day, his hair tousled and his white T-shirt clinging to his muscles— steps out of the back seat. He's carrying a half-empty water bottle in his hands again, the paper worried off it as if he spent the entire ride ripping it apart piece by piece.

I sputter at the sight of him. "What are you doing here?"

He tilts his head. "Ah yes, it's lovely to see you again too, Miss Riddle. How are you?"

Mrs. Harker and Kathleen exchange a knowing glance before heading inside.

"No, I mean—" But what am I supposed to say? That I saw Sophie post videos from his cross-country meet to her stories earlier today and mentioned getting a "well-deserved soy ice cream" with him after? I might as well just admit I'm cyber-stalking him. Although I would contend it's not stalking if her profile is *always* the first one to pop up with that brand-new pink ring around her picture because she's *always* posting. Of course, I wouldn't have known to follow her at all if hadn't cyber-stalked August in the first place, but that's just splitting hairs, really.

I quickly search for an answer that will make me sound halfway normal. "Don't you have homework?"

"A mountain of it," he says. "Don't remind me."

"So...?"

He takes a step forward, head ducked down, that slow smile that makes my knees go weak playing across his lips. "So why am I spending my Halloween in the Christmas Capital of the Universe instead of chaining myself to my desk and working on it all night?"

"Well...yeah?"

"Picking out stationery seemed more fun."

My brows arch.

He laughs. "And my dad is being a jerk. I didn't feel like getting dragged into the office for the umpteenth time this month to 'visualize where I'm going to be working in eight years' while he yells at people in Tokyo about his client's overseas transactions."

"Oh."

"Yeah."

A beat passes.

"So...are you coming too?" he asks.

"To the stationery store?"

He nods.

I hold up the candy bowl. "Someone has to hold down the fort here."

The water bottle crinkles again. "Mind if I hold down the fort with you?"

"But what about your sudden desire to pick out stationery?"

"I'm beginning to think you don't want me here, Miss Riddle."

He says it in a teasing way, but there's a layer of hurt

underneath it that has me stammering out a sharp "No!"

He blinks.

"*No*," I say quickly. "I mean—yes, I want you."

His brows threaten to disappear into his hairline.

"Here," I explain, gesturing vaguely at the sidewalk. "I want you *here*, helping me hand out candy." *Deep breath.* "I could use the company."

He sighs. "Me too."

He goes to sit on the ground next to me, but I hand him the bowl and say, "Take my chair. I'll go get another one."

I move for the door, but he hands me the bowl back.

"*I'll* go get the chair," he tells me. "I know where they are."

I narrow my eyes at him even as my heart does some seriously complicated gymnastics moves inside my chest. Why is every shape and pattern and gesture his face makes the most beautiful thing I've ever seen?

"I'm getting the chair," I tell him. "You're our guest."

"*I'm* getting the chair," he replies. "I'm a gentleman."

I roll my eyes, even though everything inside of me is screaming: *SEE? I KNEW CHIVALRY WASN'T DEAD.*

He winks, knowing he's won. "Be right back."

I watch him walk through the door and sigh.

"Um. Hello?"

I turn.

An eight-year-old Moana stares back at me.

"Can I have my candy now?" she asks.

"Oh, yeah. Here you go." I give her a packet of the chocolates we put out as wedding favors—the good ones, not those cheap ones that barely taste like chocolate you sometimes get—with *Riddle Wedding Planning* and our company tagline etched onto the ribbon. Our office phone number, email, and social media handles are also printed on it, because one of the first rules you learn when you start a small business is to turn *everything* into a marketing opportunity.

August comes back out carrying a chair, both of our moms and Kathleen following behind him.

"Don't eat all the candy, sweetheart," Mrs. Harker tells August as he sets his chair next to mine. "Save some for the kids."

"I'll do my best," he says before turning to Kathleen. "Make sure to pick out something frilly. People love frilly wedding invitations."

Kathleen rolls her eyes at him.

We watch them walk away, their bodies growing smaller and smaller until they're lost in the crowd.

Silence stretches between us.

"So," I say.

"So," he says.

I clear my throat. "A mountain of homework, huh?"

He nods. "It's nothing new. There's always a mountain. Even when you've reached the summit of one, there's another waiting just ahead."

"It must be a tough school. Our teachers love a good homework pile too, but I imagine private school must be even worse."

"They might as well call it 'Keep my kid as busy as possible so I don't have to deal with them' school," he jokes, although there's an edge to his tone that gives him away. "I guess when parents put that much money into their kids' education, they kind of expect them to be challenged."

"Otherwise, you might as well send them to public school?"

"Exactly."

I give him a pointed look.

His mouth drops. "I didn't mean to imply—there's nothing *wrong* with public school. It's just not—"

"As hard as private school?"

"Yes. I mean, no. I mean—" He leans his head back

against the top rail of his chair, rubbing his hands down his face. "Why do you do this to me, Riddle?"

"Because it's so easy, *Harker*."

"No, really." He looks over at me, completely dumbfounded. "I need to know what spell you've placed on me that turns me into a bumbling idiot every time I'm around you. I've never felt so unsure of myself in my life."

My brows arch. "*You* feel like a bumbling idiot around *me*? Excuse me, but how many times have I dropped something or almost fallen flat on my face in front of you?"

He waves off my comment. "That's just adorable. You're not making a total ass of yourself every time you're around me."

Silence.

His eyes widen as he realizes what he said. "See what I mean? I say things around you I never say to anyone else. What's that about?"

He looks genuinely confused, like he really wants an answer, but I don't have one. I'm just as mystified as he is.

"Maybe I'm your kryptonite," I say. "Maybe you should stay away from me."

Don't stay away.

His lips part, and something in his eyes shifts. My heart speeds up and my mind goes blank. I hold my breath, waiting for him to speak.

A group of kids scampers up to us, breaking the tension. They're all dressed as characters I've never seen before—some kind of neon dinosaur karate team? August sits up as I hand out the candy. They thank us and run away. I wait for August to say whatever went through his mind when I suggested he stay away from me, but he just stares out at the town square.

Moment gone.

"So," he says. "Do you think you'll go to business school

after graduation or work for your mom full time?"

"I'm not sure. I've applied to a couple places because Mom insisted, but I kind of feel like I'm getting all the business training I need just working for her. Then again, maybe I should go now so I'll know how to keep up with the business as it grows." I shrug. "Maybe I'll even learn how to generate growth we couldn't have managed otherwise."

"If it helps, the fact that you just said the words *generate growth* shows you have a real knack for this."

"I think it's just because I love weddings so much. If Mom had started a—I don't know—real estate business or an antique store or something, I don't know that we would be having the same conversation." I glance at him. "Speaking about things we love, why won't you tell your family how much you love cooking?"

"I already told you—there's no point."

"If it's your passion, you should do it. Screw what your dad thinks."

"Easy for you to say. I know you love weddings, which is convenient considering your mom's chosen career, but if you woke up tomorrow and wanted to be an—an acrobat, or a mechanic, or one of those whittlers who sell creepy wooden dolls on the side of the road, I bet your mom would support it."

"A whittler? Really?"

"You have a whittler's aura about you. I didn't mention?"

I snort. "No, you didn't."

"I think you must have been one in a previous life."

I look down at the sidewalk, at the concrete swirl patterns looping beneath my feet. "I may be able to choose anything I want, but it doesn't mean I have the ability to make it happen."

"Of course, you do. You're smart and funny and more than capable—"

"And broke."

He frowns.

"I mean, we were. Broke." I swallow. "Business is really picking up now, and we haven't had to worry about how we're going to pay our bills for a while, but almost everything we have is either going into the house or right back into the business. I'd have to take out a loan to go to college. But, you..." I shake my head at him. "You really could go anywhere. You could *pay* for anywhere."

"Actually, I can't. I know it looks that way, but it's not my money. Dad will only pay for law school. Anything else, and I'm on my own. He's made it clear I can't stay under his roof if I choose another path. So, see? I'm just as broke as you are."

"Are those designer sneakers?"

"Touché. Although, to be fair, I didn't choose them. Everyone on the team got a pair."

"And that's supposed to make it better?"

"No." He laughs. "No, that's not better at all."

"Did I just win another debate, O Captain, my captain?"

"Only because I'm going easy on you," he says, bringing his water bottle to his lips.

"So go harder."

He chokes on his water.

I cannot *believe* I just said that.

"I didn't mean—I just—Oh boy."

August throws back his head and laughs. "You're incredible, Isla Riddle. Don't ever change."

I throw a handful of candy at him. He almost falls over laughing, and I can feel it, my heart giving away bigger and bigger pieces of itself to him.

I only wish I knew how to make it stop.

9

***

Trick-or-treating ends when the sun starts to set at seven, all the kids scurrying home to dump out their treat bags. If they're anything like Evelyn, they'll color-coordinate their candies based on a best-to-worst flavor scale. If they're anything like me, they'll just take a fistful and eat until they feel sick. If they're anything like Savannah, they'll pragmatically pick a couple to keep and give the rest away because excess sugar is no friend to the brain (she usually makes a point of looking at me when she says this, and I usually smile back with a bit of chocolate stuck in my teeth).

This is the first Halloween that they haven't been here with me, and I actually kind of miss Savannah's lecture on the evils of sugar and what it does to our bodies, which is something I *never* thought I'd say. And yeah, we've all gotten so busy in the last couple years—Evelyn and Savannah with school and jobs and extracurriculars specifically chosen to help boost their college applications, and me with the business—that we hadn't gotten to hang out as much as we did when we were kids, but it's still weird, them being off at college and me being stuck here for one more year. I always knew it would be, but the reality is even harder than I imagined. Tonight, might have been unbearable if it weren't for August.

I set the candy bowl just inside the office door and lock up while August crinkles his water bottle behind me. Then we turn and head for the stationery store, him with one hand in his pocket, the other smacking his now-empty water bottle against his leg, and me crossing my arms and uncrossing them and crossing them again, feeling ridiculously aware of my own frenetic movements compared to his easygoing gait.

Why do I have to feel so awkward around him?

Just remember, a voice whispers in the back of my mind, *he says he feels just as awkward around you.*

Okay, if that's true, he does an excellent job of hiding it, and if he feels awkward, it must be because I *make* things awkward.

He has a girlfriend, I remind myself. *There's no way he's into me.*

The voice whispers back: *Isn't that what all of the heroines in the greatest romantic comedies think?*

"Oh, shut up."

August sputters. "Excuse me?"

My eyes widen. "Did I just say that out loud?"

"Uh...yeah."

I smack my hand against my face—*seriously*, how many times am I going to blush around this guy? "Sorry. I was talking to myself."

He looks amused. "I do that too."

"You do?"

"More often than usual these days."

I start walking again. "Glad I'm not the only one."

"There's actually research that shows that people who talk to themselves are geniuses," he says, keeping pace with me.

"Then I must be the next Marie Curie."

"And I must be the next Albert Einstein."

I hold my hand out. "Nice to meet you, Albert."

August's palm grazes mine, his eyes sparkling in the twilight. "Nice to meet you, Marie."

We hold hands a second too long, and then we're both clearing our throats and looking away from each other.

"So," August says, crinkling his water bottle again. "Where is this store?"

I glance up, suddenly realizing I wasn't paying attention to where we were going. "Oh, right there. Across the street."

We wait for a car to pass before crossing, August's sneakers and my ballet flats slapping the pavement. The sign on the door says the shop closes at seven, but through the bay window we spy Kathleen and our moms still engrossed in a pile of invitation options, debating back and forth among themselves.

A bell over the door tinkles as we walk in.

"Darling," Mrs. Harker calls out, spotting August. "How did it go? Were there a lot of trick-or-treaters?"

"At least a hundred."

He's not joking. I lost count of how many Elsas and Spider-Mans we saw.

"How's it going here?" he asks.

"We've narrowed it down to five options, but I really don't know how we're going to choose," Kathleen says, her head in her hands. "Can I see the ivory with the cream backdrop again?"

Madeline, the owner of the store, patiently unearths the invitation.

Kathleen shakes her head. "I just can't decide if I prefer

this one to the eggshell and pearl."

"My vote is for the deep cranberry with the snowflake edging along the insert," Mrs. Harker says. "Red is perfect for a Christmas wedding."

Kathleen groans. "Why is this so difficult?"

"You know, I think we may be here a little while longer," Mom says, meeting my gaze. "Why don't you and August grab everyone some coffees?"

"Of course," I say. "Decaf?"

Mom and Mrs. Harker nod.

Kathleen says, "Make mine a double espresso."

August and I exchange a look.

"Extra shot of nervous energy, coming up," he says, following me to the door.

The bell tinkles once more as we head back outside.

"She's not usually like this," he says as the door closes behind him. "She just wants it to be perfect. She's been dreaming about this her whole life."

"You don't have to explain it to me," I assure him. "Every bride we've ever had just wants their wedding to be perfect. That's why they hire a wedding planner. And trust me, your sister is far from a Bridezilla. We once had a bride change her wedding colors half a dozen times and then tried to change them one more time *a week before the wedding.*"

August looks mortified. "Like, the bridesmaid dresses and the tuxes and—and everything?"

"YES."

He rubs his chest. "I know I haven't been doing this whole wedding-planning thing for very long, but that gives me a panic attack just thinking about it."

"Trust me, it took a lot of convincing on my mom's part to talk her out of it. But the amazing thing is that, on the wedding day, all she could say was how beautiful everything looked. She was like a completely different person, just enjoying the moment. I wish I could say all of our brides are like that, but some are still giant stress balls the entire day of the wedding."

"I hope Kathleen isn't."

"She won't be."

"How can you tell?"

"I have a sixth sense about these things. She'll be cool as a cucumber the second she walks down the aisle."

August looks relieved.

We head down the street and into the coffee shop. We place our order, then head for the only table left, next to the window. August flicks his twisted-up water bottle against the side of the table as he studies the town square, where volunteers are already taking down the Halloween decorations—the scarecrows and the cornstalks and the autumn wreaths—and replacing them with even more red bows and garland than were there previously.

"You know, there's a recycling can behind you," I tell him. "If you wanted to get rid of that thing."

August stops mid-flick. "Sorry. Old habit."

"It doesn't bother me."

"Really?"

I nod because I actually find it ridiculously cute. I want to ask him why he does it, where it came from, how it started, but I don't want to make him self-conscious.

"Sophie hates it," he says. "She's always ripping them out of my hands and throwing them away. She can't stand the crinkling noise it makes. Drives her up a wall."

Sophie drives *me* up a wall.

I fold my hands on the table. "You know what I think you should do?"

He shakes his head.

"Keep another one in your pocket. That way when she throws away the first, you can pull out a fresh one."

He laughs. "That's perfect. That would definitely do her in."

Or, you know, you could just break up with her.

I wince. I really need to stop thinking things like that, considering THEY SOMETIMES ACTUALLY COME OUT OF MY MOUTH.

Thank God I don't say that one out loud.

Did I?

"Are they really putting Christmas decorations up already?" August asks, gesturing out the window.

No. I definitely didn't.

"We take Christmas very seriously in this town," I explain.

"They do realize there's still one more holiday before Christmas, right?"

"Why, whatever could you mean, dear stranger of the North?"

"Oh, you know, that little American tradition we like to call *Thanksgiving*?"

"You mean Practice Christmas?"

He shakes his head, grinning. "This town really is something."

"I know. I love it so much." I lean back in my chair. "Tourism really starts to ramp up in November, but since so many of the people here benefit from the tourist economy, we play up the Christmas angle in some way or another all year long. We put on a great Christmas-in-July festival too." I try to make it sound like it doesn't really matter to me one way or another as I add, "You should come."

He leans forward, crossing his arms on the table. "Only if you show me around."

"Y-yeah. Okay."

August smiles. He looks like he's about to say something else, but then his gaze drifts to a table behind me. "What's their deal?"

I glance over my shoulder. Three of the most popular girls in school—Layla Ashton, Maia Brooks, and Kennedy McCade—are all sitting huddled together, darting looks at our table and laugh-whispering at each other.

"Oh, them." I wave it off like it's nothing, even though the menace in their eyes feels like knives slowly flaying my skin. "They're probably just wondering why someone like you is sitting with someone like me."

He looks confused.

"You know, because you're"—my cheeks warm—"um, physically well-inclined, and I'm sort of...average?"

"That's the most ridiculous thing I've ever heard."

"It's okay," I say quickly. "I would wonder why you were with me too, if I was them."

"You really don't have a clue how beautiful you are, do you?" He shakes his head. "Isla, you're a knockout."

I open my mouth. Close it. Open it again. I probably look like that horrible singing fish people keep in their offices, but I literally cannot think of a single thing to say in response to that.

Thankfully, August is too busy glaring at Layla, Maia, and Kennedy to notice. "I'll settle this."

He grabs all the pink sugar packets from our table and stuffs them into his pocket. He's halfway to their table before my brain even registers the fact that he's left.

"What are you doing?" I whisper at his back.

He waves off my question with a flick of his hand. I sink down in my chair and watch through a slim opening between my hands, mortified.

"Hey there," August says once he gets to their table.

All three girls go all doe-eyed. Layla crosses her forearms on the table, pushing her breasts up against them.

"Hi," she says in a fake-breathy voice.

I roll my eyes.

"Could I borrow a sugar packet?" he asks. "See, my *girlfriend* over there"—he looks at me and smiles—"well, she just can't drink her coffee without one, and as you can see, our table is all out."

OH MY SUGARPLUM FAIRIES, DID HE REALLY JUST SAY THAT OUT LOUD?

The girls look just as shocked as I feel as they hand him a sugar packet.

He winks. "Thanks."

"This can't be my life," I murmur as he sits back down across from me, flinging the sugar packet onto the table.

August wriggles his eyebrows. "And yet it is."

Oh sure, NOW words come out of my mouth.

He leans back in his seat, replacing all of the sugar packets—the mean girls start whispering again—and says, "Seriously, Isla. You're amazing, inside *and* out, and don't let anyone ever tell you any differently, especially not a bunch of girls who are clearly just jealous of you."

I cross my arms. "If they're jealous of anything, it's that I'm here with you."

"And if those guys over there"—he points to a group of boys I recognize from school, working on a project and also darting glances over at our table—"are jealous of anything, it's that *I'm* here with *you*."

"Those guys? No way."

"Any of them ever ask you out before?"

I look back at them. "Well, I went to Homecoming with Logan, and Eli asked me out to a football game once, but I was working a wedding. And—"

I cut myself off, suddenly realizing something.

"And?" August asks.

"They've all asked me out a couple times, but I had to say no because all of my weekends are taken up by weddings. And then they just...stopped asking."

"See?" He arches a brow. "They're into you. They just don't think you're into them."

"That's because I'm not."

He gives me a pointed look.

"I mean, they're nice guys," I explain. "They're just not my type."

"And what *is* your type, Miss Riddle?"

You.

"I'm not sure."

He raps his knuckles on the table, his water bottle sitting forgotten next to the now-disheveled sugar packets. "Well, when you figure it out, let me know. I'll be on the lookout."

"Thanks."

"Don't mention it."

The waitress brings our coffees over in a to-go carrier. I grab mine, pop off the lid, and add the sugar packet, pointedly glancing at Layla, Maia, and Kennedy before lifting the coffee up in a *cheers* gesture.

August snorts.

"For future reference," I tell him as we stand. "I hate sugar in my coffee."

He gives me his brightest smile, the one that seems to be coming out more and more whenever he's around me.

"I'll remember that," he says.

And then he grabs my hand and tugs me possessively into him. I know he's just trying to prove a point to those girls, but for the twelve steps it takes for us to walk out of the coffee shop and out of their view, with his arm wrapped around me and my ribcage flush against his own, I feel like the luckiest girl in the world to be so close to a boy who could literally have any girl he wanted and for a smidgen of a moment—even if none of it was real—he chose me.

10

***

I try to focus on my English paper—one thousand words on the major themes of *Our Town*—but my mind keeps drifting back to a coffee shop and a sugar packet and the words *"You're a knockout"* falling so easily from August's perpetually curving lips. I can't stop thinking about how every molecule in my body comes alive whenever he's around. Can't stop wondering if that's how he feels when he's with Sophie or if Beckett's right—if the lack of smiling in Sophie's pictures says more than a thousand words ever could.

If she doesn't make you smile—if she makes the stars fall from your eyes—then yet again, I ask: why are you with her?

And then there's that blasted pink ring around Sophie's stories again, and I know I shouldn't click on it, I know I should just let it go, but I'm desperate for another sight of him, even if that sight comes from the lens of *her* camera. I click on her stories, swiping through some pictures she took at cheerleading practice, until I get to pictures from a Halloween party. Sophie is wearing a skin-tight Catwoman costume, and all sorts of guys are crowding around her, drooling over her shiny pleather bodysuit. I keep swiping through, picture after picture, but I don't see a single sign of August anywhere.

Maybe he's taking the pictures?

The second-to-last shot is one of Sophie jutting out her lower lip in a sad-pouty way, with loopy text written across the top that reads, *What do you do when your boyfriend chooses homework over you?* I swipe to the last story. It's a video of all the guys taking their shirts off and *Magic Mike*–dancing around Sophie, while she just stands there, arms crossed and looking smug as all get-out, with the words *MAKE HIM JEALOUS* in red-hot, capital letters written across the top with a fire emoji.

Wow. Just...wow.

I mean, I know I've never actually dated anyone before, but I've watched enough rom-coms to know manipulation is never the key to a successful relationship.

Maybe that means they won't be in a relationship much longer.

The hope that wells up inside of me at that thought is almost too painful to bear.

I try to go back to my paper, but I keep wondering if August has seen Sophie's stories and what he thinks about them. *Is* it making him jealous? Or is it making him wonder why he's with her? And then, it hits me: He could have done his homework and then gone to the party. Instead, he chose to do his homework later so he could come to the office with Kathleen, and while I know, logically, that it's probably just because he wants to spend as much time with her as possible before she moves to London, another part of me is thinking about the fact that every time we've been together, he's spent more time with me than with either his mom or Kathleen.

Is it possible August chose me over Sophie tonight?

My phone buzzes. A text from an unknown number.

Sorry again about the sugar packet. I hope the coffee was bearable.

I drop my phone.

Pick it back up.

August? I type back.

He sends back a winky face, and why does a single emoji from him cause my heart to leap out of my chest in the exact same way it does whenever he throws an actual wink my way?

Me: *How did you get my number?*

August: *It's on the emergency contact list in Kathleen's wedding packet. I hope that's okay.*

I tuck my feet up onto my desk chair, knees in my chest.

Me: *That depends. What's the emergency?*

August: *I've been thinking a lot about what you said earlier, and I want to change the wedding colors. I know I'm not the bride and may not have the proper authorization to do that, but come on, Christmas colors for a Christmas wedding? A little obvious, don't you think?*

My smile widens.

Me: *What did you have in mind?*

August: *I'm thinking we go with an "under the sea" theme. Seaweed, little plastic crabs on the tables, the whole nine yards.*

Me: *Don't you mean the whole nine nautical miles?*

August: *Damn, you're smart. I'm not sure I can keep talking to someone who's smarter than me. I might lose my street cred.*

Me: *Did you have any to begin with?*

August: *Ouch, Riddle. I do have feelings, you know.*

Me: *<laughing emoji> Sorry.*

August: *No, no, it's okay. The truth hurts.*

Three dots appear, and I lean forward, holding my breath, waiting for his next words.

August: *What are you doing right now?*

Me: *Homework.*

I almost ask him about the party but send a *You?* instead. Probably better he doesn't know I'm cyber-stalking him through his girlfriend.

August: *Just finished.*

A pause.

The three dots appear again.

August: *Any chance I can convince you to stop what you're doing and watch a movie with me?*

I swallow.

Me: *What movie?*

August: *Two Weeks Notice is streaming. I've never seen it.*

Me: *You haven't?*

August: *Want to stream it with me? Be my rom-com movie guide?*

Me: *YES.*

Crap. Should I have put it in all capital letters like that? Am I being overly enthusiastic? Will he be able to tell I'm falling in love with him from that one overly emphasized word alone?

But all he texts back is the word *Excellent* with a winky face, and I feel like I can breathe again.

I head down the hall, passing Mom's room. Her door is open. She's fallen asleep on top of her covers, her laptop propped against her knees. I close the laptop and set it on her desk, then slide off her glasses, tuck a spare blanket over her, and turn off her light. I close the door quietly behind me before practically skipping into the family room, clicking on the side-table lamp and plopping down onto the couch. I grab the remote and scroll until I find the movie. I'm about to text, *Ready?* but then my phone rings.

August.

Hands shaking, I hit the Answer button. "Hello?"

"Hey."

I can hear the smile on his lips, the faint hush of his breath across the receiver.

"Hi," I say back.

"Thanks for watching this with me. I couldn't sleep."

And I feel all warm and gooey inside because I know he could be at that party with Sophie, but just like earlier tonight, for some reason I can't comprehend, he's choosing me instead.

"You're in for a treat," I tell him. "It's my second-favorite Hugh Grant movie."

"What's your first?"

"*Notting Hill.*"

"A classic."

"Also impossible to beat. 'I'm just a girl, standing in front of a boy, asking him to love her?' Who can outdo that?"

"Well, our current challenger is Miss Sandra Bullock, whom I must say is quite the wordsmith herself."

I settle into the side of the couch and force myself to focus on the movie, even though I'd be happy just listening to the way he breathes and the way he laughs and the way he makes snarky comments about Hugh Grant's closet.

"Who actually needs their clothes to revolve around like that? He might as well write the word *A-HOLE* on his forehead in permanent marker and be done with it."

"Are you telling me your closet doesn't do that?" I tease. "And here I thought you were rich."

"Not that rich apparently."

"Oh yes. Only private-plane-and-yacht rich, not revolving-closet rich. My mistake."

We laugh and we joke, and we make deep comments

about the pros and cons of capitalism, and suddenly it's two hours later. I don't want to get off the phone even though the credits are rolling and it's one o'clock in the morning and if I don't go to bed soon, I'm going to seriously regret it when my alarm clock goes off.

"I should let you go," he says, his voice thick, his words slow, as if he's finding it harder and harder to keep his eyes open.

I'm curled up on the couch, my chest pressing into my knees, my knees pressing into the cushions, and I know I could fall asleep so easily like this, listening to the sleepy cadence of his voice.

"What time do you get up for school?" I ask.

"Six. You?"

"Same."

"Mind if I text you again? You know, in case I get some deep revelation about revolving closets while I sleep?"

My heart flutters. "Text away."

"Excellent." He inhales. "Good night, Isla Riddle."

"Good night, August Harker."

II

✳✳✳

August and I text each other all week. First, he goes through Hugh Grant's entire IMDB page, comparing and contrasting his movies with me. Then we move on to talking about school and cross-country meets and how much he hates the locker-room talk he hears. He actually told some guy to shove it when he overheard him bragging about something he did with a girl in their class, and then he immediately texted me that his adrenaline was through the roof and where was an empty water bottle when he needed one?

Me: *Is that why you carry them? To crinkle out the adrenaline?*

August: *Adrenaline. Nerves. Anxiety. It's good for a myriad of things.*

Me: *Myriad. Nice SAT word.*

August: *Thanks. I've been practicing. <winky-face emoji>*

I tell him about how much I miss Evelyn and Savannah, especially in the cafeteria when I have to sit with people I don't really like just so I don't have to sit alone. He tells me about how much he'll miss Kathleen—how when they were younger, and his dad was always working and their mom was always at some social event or another, they formed this really tight bond, even though Kathleen's five years older than he is. He says it was weird in the house when she was off at college but it's going to be even worse now that she won't be coming home on school breaks.

Me: *Yeah, but you can always visit her in London. How amazing would that be?*

August: *Okay, yeah. London's pretty cool.*

Me: *Wait—you've actually BEEN to London?*

August: *Only two or three times a year. My dad has an office there, remember?*

Me: *JEALOUS. I've always wanted to visit England. And Scotland. And Ireland. Pretty much all the "lands".*

Three dots appear as August types.

Then they vanish.

Then they appear again.

I hold my breath and think, *Say it. Whatever you want to say. Just say it.*

August: *Maybe if we're ever there at the same time...I could show you around?*

Me: *What would you show me?*

A beat passes.

My heart flutters, waiting for his response.

August: *Everything.*

✱✱✱

On Friday, Mom and I get a call from Kathleen that she wants to change her reception venue from the family's country club to the Gallica Botanical Conservatory, located exactly halfway between Christmas and Richmond. "Josh surprised me with a picnic in the Rainforest Room during his lunch break yesterday, and I just fell in love with the space. Is it too late to change?"

Mom and I have never been to the conservatory before—we've never had a bride with a big enough budget to even consider it—but when I mention it to August, he says it's incredible. Like walking into a dream.

Thankfully, the Harkers are able to get their deposit back from the country club, being founding members and all, and we manage to book a tour of the space on Saturday, right after the cake tasting we already had scheduled in Richmond.

August texts me Saturday morning that he can't make the cake tasting—cross-country practice—but he'll be at the conservatory. He asks me to save him some cake. I grab him a piece of double fudge chocolate because I remember him telling me a perfect world in his mind would be one entirely made of chocolate, to which I told him I wholeheartedly agreed.

Now, Mom and I are touring the second of three possible reception spaces in the conservatory with Kathleen and Mrs. Harker leading the way as they listen to the conservatory's event planner describing receptions they've held in the past, and I keep checking my phone, wondering when August will get here. I almost check Sophie's stories to see if he's with her, but I unfollowed her after August started texting me every day. I want updates to come directly from him—his voice, his fingertips, his words—not filtered snapshots viewed through her camera lens.

I can be patient.

Look, another minute has gone by, and I haven't even checked my phone.

And another minute.

Nope. Fifteen seconds.

Why does time move so slow when I'm waiting to hear from him?

You're in love.

No, I'm not.

Yes, you are. You just don't want to admit it because he may be texting you, but he's with her.

Oh, would you just SHUT UP?

Everyone looks at me.

"Did you say something, honey?" Mom asks.

I shake my head, my lips forming a tight line. "Nope."

I have GOT to stop doing that.

We step into the third possible reception space—the Rainforest Room that Kathleen fell in love with during her picnic with her fiancé. Waterfalls cascade down rocks into ponds hidden by massive jungle foliage. Trees tower over us, weaving an emerald canopy through which bands of diffused sunlight create a soft green glow over everything, and the most beautiful burgundy, fuchsia, indigo, and sapphire flowers alight on lily pads and drip from vines. It's breathtaking, but there's nothing "Christmas" about it, and the small, winding paths are much too narrow for a reception party of her size.

Thankfully, I don't have to point out the obvious. Mom's already breaking it to Kathleen, suggesting it as an excellent option for the wine bar and hors d'oeuvres station, while explaining that the opulent Glass Room—a space as big as a ballroom with glass walls so thin, it looks like they aren't even there at all—would actually make for the best reception space, especially as the conservatory is already in the process of lining the room with pine trees for Christmas. All we'll have to do is add extra twinkle lights and lanterns to really give it that "enchanted winter forest" vibe that we've already chosen for the church.

I'm taking notes for Mom on my phone—Daphne's

heading the setup of another wedding that we'll go to from here—when I suddenly feel a rush of breath against my ear.

"Hey," August whispers.

My whole body tingles in response and, for just a moment, I lean into him, into the crook of his shoulder, the side of his body melding against mine, but I have enough sense to move away quickly, as if I were only ever just turning, greeting his smile with my own.

I place my phone in my back pocket and pull the little brown box out of the oversized, black leather bag I use on wedding days. If August were to peek inside of it, he would find a plastic box holding a rainbow of thread options; double-sided tape; makeup remover; an unopened, travel-sized stick of deodorant (for the nervous bride in need of extra applications throughout the day); granola bars for the hungry brides and mini water bottles for the thirsty ones; tissues; stain remover; lint roller; Band-Aids; shoe inserts; and even supportive pasties for those brides (or bridesmaids) who can't wear a bra with their dress but really need one. There's also a printed schedule and checklist in case my phone dies or gets lost or stolen, because while most people would instantly freak out if they lost their phone and drop everything to find it, a wedding planner cannot drop anything. The wedding must keep moving until the very last guest has left and the bride and groom are well on their way to wedded bliss, and if a phone is lost forever in the process, so be it.

"I offer you your cake, good sir," I tell him, handing him the box.

He opens it, then throws back his head and makes a grateful, guttural sound in the back of his throat. "Thank you."

"You're welcome."

"Actually, I was thanking God for inventing chocolate." He smiles. "*Now* I'm thanking you."

"Darling," Mrs. Harker says, pulling August into a hug. "How was practice?"

"Great," August says, picking up the tiny plastic spoon and swirling it through the cake's gooey chocolate middle. "The whole team shaved at least a minute off their best times."

"That's wonderful."

August takes a bite and groans again. "Not as wonderful as this cake. Please tell me Kathleen picked this one."

Mom shakes her head. "She chose vanilla with white fondant."

"But that's like"—August sputters—"the most boring of cakes."

"Also the most likely to be enjoyed by everyone," Mrs. Harker points out.

August glances at me, looking so disappointed all I want to do is give him a hug. "Please tell me she's joking."

Mrs. Harker shakes her head and chuckles under her breath as she goes back to Mom and Kathleen.

August grabs my arm, feigning desperation. "You have to help me change my sister's mind about the cake."

"And if I don't?" I tease.

"You must help me, madam. My future happiness is at stake!"

"I don't think we're going to change her mind, but maybe I could take you back there sometime? We could grab cake and coffee, and then you can try all of their chocolate options. There were at least seventeen of them."

His smile freezes.

Oh no. Oh no, oh no, *oh no.*

Did I just accidentally ask August out on a date?

Okay, deep breaths. This isn't that bad. Sure, you somehow let your flirtatious texts carry over into real life and now he's looking at you like you've sprouted three heads, but you can fix this—right?

"That would be..." August clears his throat, trying to figure out how to let me down easy.

FIX IT, FIX IT, FIX—

"You could bring your girlfriend," I say quickly, the words rushing out of my mouth before I even know what I'm saying, "and I could bring my boyfriend, and we could double-date. It'll be fun."

August's brow furrows. "You have a boyfriend?"

NO. I HAVE NO IDEA WHY I SAID THAT.

I nod. "His name's Ryan. Ryan Mulcahy. It's new. As of... yesterday. I didn't mention it?"

He swallows. "No. You didn't."

"Yeah. He's liked me for a while, and I remembered what you said at the coffee shop, and I thought, you know, that maybe you were right? That maybe it was time I try this whole 'dating thing' out?"

STOP. TALKING.

August stares at the floor.

I bump his shoulder. "It also gets you off the hook."

He glances up. "How do you mean?"

"Well, you don't have to be on the lookout for me anymore. I'm taken."

"And you"—he exhales—"you like this Ryan guy?"

I shrug. "He's captain of the football team and he's in the National Honor Society." *And he's completely made up.* "What's not to like?"

August scratches the back of his head, the cake box sitting in his other hand, completely forgotten. "Um, yeah. A double date. That sounds great."

"Wonderful."

He stares at his shoes. "Fantastic." But something about the way he says it makes me think he doesn't think it's fantastic at all.

I look over at Mom, who's busy painting a verbal picture of décor ideas and table placements for Kathleen and Mrs. Harker.

"I should probably get back over there," I tell him, starting forward.

August's hand wraps around my arm. "Wait."

I look back at him.

"Play hooky with me?" he asks.

"I don't think I can—"

"Just for a few minutes? You've never been here before, right?"

I shake my head.

When his smile comes, it's slow, inching up his face in the most adorable way, like a little boy who's only just realized it's Christmas morning. "There's something I want to show you."

I glance at Mom, Kathleen, and Mrs. Harker. They're all turned away from us, completely oblivious to anything but the vision Mom is creating of Kathleen's dream wedding.

"Fine," I tell him. "But we can't be long."

"Don't worry," he says, setting the cake box on a bench and taking my hand. "It's not far."

12

***

He holds my hand the entire way.

I don't think he thought anything of it at first, but halfway across the room, he must feel the way my body stiffens, every ounce of my being focused intently on the warmth of his palm against mine, because his body tenses too, and then, as if coming to a decision, as if he doesn't have a girlfriend and I don't have a (pretend) boyfriend, his grip tightens, and he looks at me, his eyes shaping the question *Is this okay?*

I squeeze his hand in confirmation, my pulse pounding in my ears.

He adjusts his grip, deliberately folding his hand around mine as he leads me out of the Glass Room and into the Rainforest Room, through the Desert Room and around the orchid-butterfly house. I think we're going to veer left, continuing on the main path, but there's a small opening to the right, nearly hidden by a curtain of diamond-shaped leaves, and he pushes them aside to let me through.

The path gets narrower, foliage spilling onto brick pavers, until we duck through an archway in a black volcanic rock wall that makes me feel like we're stepping into a cave. The archway opens into a small room that's just a bridge over a pond with the same black volcanic walls surrounding us, covered in vines. A waterfall spills into the pond, where lily pads dot the dark water's placid surface and a glass ceiling arcs over us, painted gray by the November sky.

We stop in the middle of the bridge.

"Do you know what those are?" August asks, gesturing to the vines.

I shake my head.

"Moonflowers." He leans his forearms against the bridge's railing. I mimic his pose. "They bloom at night and glow in the light of a full moon."

"Wow," I say, my gaze wandering around the room at the closed, green buds sprouting from the vines. "That must be incredible. Have you ever seen them?"

He shakes his head. "I haven't been here since a class field trip in the eighth grade. I was so fascinated by this plant in the other room that I didn't realize my class had gone on without me, but when I got to the veer in the path, I took the smaller one, thinking maybe it was a shortcut or something."

"And you ended up in here?"

He nods. "I would've stayed in this room the entire field trip and after too, if I thought I could get away with it. I got the feeling that this is a sort of secret garden in the conservatory—not too many people find it, and the staff doesn't advertise it. It's like a special surprise for people who are willing to look for it, and I was afraid if I stayed too long, the entire class would come looking for me and then they would stumble onto this place, and all of the magic would disappear if it wasn't a secret anymore. If it wasn't *mine* anymore." He taps his fingers on the railing, probably wishing it was a water bottle he was tapping instead. "I was a pretty selfish thirteen-year-old, huh?"

"I don't think it's selfish to want something this magical to have been made just for you. It's what everyone wants, right? To be special?"

His reflection chews on his bottom lip, his brows sweeping low over his eyes as he gazes at me in the water. "But I shouldn't feel that way. You said it yourself. I'm private-plane rich. I want for nothing."

"Nothing but a revolving closet."

"Don't remind me."

I shift my weight, my shoulder brushing his.

I don't move.

He doesn't either.

"Just because you come from a rich family," I tell him, my voice hushed in this space so obviously created for tranquility, "doesn't mean you don't know want. Your dad isn't exactly letting you chase after your own dreams."

August shifts, and now our forearms are touching. Our wrists. The sides of our hands as they curve over the railing. He grits his teeth at the contact, almost as if it's physically painful for him, but he doesn't move away. "No one in my life gets why that should bother me so much. Not when I have this path placed in front of me that so many people would kill for."

I swallow, thinking about how natural he looked in Caio's kitchen, all smooth lines and flicking wrists and dancing knives and swirling spoons. I've never been so mesmerized by a person's hands; how quick and efficient they can be. How gently they can cradle something as small and delicate as a scallop. How firmly they can grip the handle of a whisk, veins bulging down tanned forearms as ingredients circle and blend at the bottom of a saucepan.

"I get it," I whisper.

We aren't staring at our reflections anymore. We're staring at our hands, and all I want is for him to slide his palm across my palm again. To tangle his fingers with mine. To touch me on purpose.

Instead, he pushes away from the railing.

Cold air rushes in where his warmth disappeared.

"You know, the reception is going to be at night. And I checked the lunar calendar." He meets my gaze. "It's going to be a full moon."

I swear under my breath.

"Okay," he says, laughing. "Not the reaction I expected."

"Sorry, it's just...people can get weird around full moons. They don't always bode well for big events."

"No, but they do bode well for seeing moonflowers glow."

"Oh." I glance around at the vines, wondering what it would be like to see hundreds of moonflowers all glowing at once. "I hadn't thought of that."

"So, how about it? Want to sneak away with me that night and check them out?"

Yes.

"What if it's cloudy?" I ask, my mouth suddenly dry.

"Looks like they provide for that," he says, tilting his head up, where strategically placed purple, blue, and green spotlights are stationed in the corners of the room.

"What about Sophie?"

I saw the finalized guest list last night. Sophie's name was on it, and it was requested that she be seated at the family's table.

"Sophie won't mind. She'll be too busy taking selfies and hitting on waiters." He gives me that adorable half smirk, but it doesn't quite reach his eyes. "The better question is—what about Ryan?"

"Ryan who?"

His brow arches. "Your boyfriend?"

I need to tell him. It's going to be terrible and awkward and I'm going to look like the biggest freak, but I can't keep pretending I have a boyfriend just because he made me want to crawl under a rock when I inadvertently asked him out.

But when I open my mouth, the words "Oh, yeah. Sorry. It's new," come out instead.

And the hole just keeps getting deeper.

"As of yesterday," August reminds me.

"Right." I take a deep breath. For better or for worse, I'm in it now. And maybe it's a good thing to have a reason to stop crushing so hard on a boy who will never love me back, even if that reason is as fake as those multicolored lights set up to replace the moon's glow. "No, I don't think he'll mind."

"Great. We'll make our escape when everyone's distracted." He places his hands in his pockets in that relaxed pose that I love so much. "I'll be the one in a tux."

"I'll be the one with a headset."

He laughs and bumps my shoulder. "Come on. Time to get you back."

We don't hold hands this time. He keeps his hands in his pockets. I cross my arms. And the space between us feels larger somehow than just the few inches of air separating our shoulders. It feels like something has been lost, something fragile, but I can't say what. All I know is that I never again want to see him look at me the way he did when I asked him to go back to the bakery with me—like I'm Julia Roberts, standing in front of my own Hugh Grant, asking him to love me, but he's already happy with Sandra Bullock, and my pleas are falling on deaf ears.

13

***

Mom, Kathleen, and Mrs. Harker are still talking when we get back, and August arches a brow at me like, *See? They didn't even notice we were gone.* And it seems like he's right—at least it does until Mom and I are back in our car, heading home to Christmas for a sunset ceremony in the Methodist church on Mulberry, followed by a reception in the public library's art deco event space. That's when Mom gives me *the look*, and I know what's coming before she even speaks.

"So," she says, her tone half-suspicious, half-amused, "where did you and August sneak off to?"

I wince. "Sorry. Did I miss anything important?"

"No worries. I've got all the reception details up here," she says, pointing to her temple. Then: "You two seem to enjoy running off together."

I let my head fall back against the seat as I gaze out the rain-dotted window at the trees passing by. They bend and sway in the wind, their crowns burnished with autumn fire. "It's not what you think. He has a girlfriend."

"That doesn't mean it's not what I think."

"Okay, then. What do you think?"

She glances at me. "I think you like him."

I don't say anything.

"And I think he likes you."

"Yeah, right."

"Why is that so hard to believe?"

"Have you seen his girlfriend?"

"No," Mom says, turning onto the interstate. "But I've seen *you*. And I've seen the way he looks at you."

"We're just friends."

Mom makes a *hmm* sound in the back of her throat. "Just do me a favor and let me know when his title changes from 'friend' to 'boyfriend' so I can set some ground rules, okay?"

"MOM."

"Ground rules are important, honey. You never know what kind of trouble those wily teenage hormones can get you into."

My phone buzzes with a text before I can tell her how far off base she is.

August: *Finally finishing my cake. Sorry I was kind of a jerk about it earlier. I would love nothing more than to go on a double date with you and New Boyfriend Ryan if it means I get to eat this cake again.*

I'm trying to think of what I should say when the three dots appear, then disappear, then appear again. My breath always catches when he does this, wondering what he was going to say before he decided to erase it.

August: *Just hit me up whenever.*

Hit him up? I don't like how final that sounds, like I'm not supposed to text him again until I have a concrete plan. Ugh, why does texting a boy you like have to be so hard?

Me: *Cool. Will do.*

There. Nice, casual, breezy, and in no way hinting at the sudden despair I feel at the thought that I won't hear from August again until I've figured out how to go on a double date with him and Sophie and *my pretend boyfriend, Ryan.*

I squeeze my eyes shut.

My phone buzzes again.

August: *Shall we continue dissecting Hugh Grant movies tonight? I see Nine Months is also streaming.*

I let out a huge breath. Mom gives me a sidelong look, but I don't care because August still wants to watch movies with me and text me about his day and show me the bits and pieces of himself that hide underneath the veneer he puts on for everyone else. I didn't completely ruin whatever our relationship is by accidentally asking him out on a date. If anything, I saved it by making up Fake Boyfriend Ryan.

Maybe I should write a dating manual.

Me: *Wow.*

August: *?*

Me: *You've actually discovered a rom-com I haven't seen.*

August: *You're joking.*

Me: *Nope. It's on my list, but I haven't gotten around to it. Haven't had a whole lot of time since Mom started the business.*

August: *Okay. We're definitely watching it, then.*

Me: *What time?*

August: *8?*

Me: *I'll be at the reception until 11.*

August: *I'll still be up at 11.*

I almost type, *It's a date,* then backspace. I wonder what he thinks when he sees the three dots appear and disappear and appear again. Wonder if it makes his own heart ratchet up into his throat, wishing he knew the words I decided were too revealing to share.

Me: *Call you then.*

He sends back a dancing GIF and it practically makes my heart burst because he's free. Tonight. On a Saturday night. And he's choosing to spend it watching a rom-com with me. My face lights up brighter than a thousand-watt Christmas tree. I try to hide it, but it's like trying to hide the sun when there isn't a single cloud in the sky.

Mom shakes her head. "Oh yeah. There's nothing going on between the two of you *at all.*"

14

***

I haven't seen August in two weeks, and a world without his smile is a million percent dimmer.

It helps that we've been texting almost nonstop—in the morning before school; in between classes; after school, when he's getting ready for practice and I'm on my way to the office. One day he texts me a picture of a chipmunk that found its way into the boys' locker room, but he was facing a mirror, so along with the adorable chipmunk I got a full view of August's abs reflected in the glass, and I haven't been able to get the image of his muscles out of my head ever since.

But our nighttime conversations are my favorite, when I can actually hear his voice, his breath, his laughter, every part and parcel of me humming in response, like the echo of a bell thrumming long after it has been struck. The second I get home from the office, I speed through whatever homework I wasn't able to get done during lunch, just so that I can have more time on the phone with him.

We've watched a movie every single night (*How to Lose a Guy in 10 Days, Sleepless in Seattle, Say Anything, 10 Things I Hate About You,* and *The Breakfast Club*—technically not a romantic comedy, but a movie we both agree is solidly in the Top Five Movies Ever Made category), and it's starting to scare me—how hard I'm falling for him. For the sound of his voice in my ear. For the anticipation of his texts. For the way I can hear his smile through the phone as his breath catches when I say something funny, and for the way he's helped me to access that part of myself, that witty, confident side that only Mom, Evelyn, and Savannah have ever seen.

I'm terrified of what will happen when we no longer have reasons to text. When the wedding is over, and August has no need of the girl who sometimes made him laugh. When he and Sophie fly off into the sunset together on his family's private plane and the magic that has wrapped around these past few weeks of my life disappears for good, just like those ever-maddening three dots on my phone.

In almost every rom-com I've ever watched, if the heroine is dating anyone at all when the movie starts, it's always the Wrong Guy, and it's so *clearly* the Wrong Guy to both her and to the audience that there isn't even a shred of heartbreak when their relationship ends and the Right Guy walks into her life.

But what do you do when the Right Guy is the one who breaks your heart?

That's my biggest fear. That no one else could ever compare to August Harker.

Mom and I have been busy finalizing vendors, mailing invitations, and making sure all the bridesmaids have been fitted for their dresses. The slightly warmer days of early November have faded, and the leaves have begun to fall, lining the sidewalks of our town in a crunchy orange-red blanket. We've also had four new brides come in for consultations and details on six upcoming weddings to figure out. Every afternoon, August texts me the most ridiculous ideas for wedding themes he can think of, and I tell him that if the culinary school thing doesn't pan out, he should definitely come work for us.

Every once in a while, he asks about Fake Ryan, and I tell him we grabbed coffee when we didn't, or that he walked me to work when I walked by myself, and I feel like I'm shrinking with every lie. Soon Mom's going to be able to carry me around in her purse and tell people about how she used to have a daughter but now she has a Polly Pocket. But the lie has gotten so big, I have no idea how to get out of it. Plus, it makes all this texting easier. If he believes I'm in a relationship, he won't think I'm trying to be anything more than his friend. If he thinks I'm not in a relationship, then that weirdness that happened between us at the conservatory will come back, and what if he stops texting me because of it?

I know it will have to stop eventually, but I'm just not ready to give him up yet. And with Evelyn and Savannah away at college, one of them busy with a boyfriend and the other busy with an extra-credit archaeological dig site, August has become more than just the boy I'm falling for these past few weeks.

He's become my best friend.

I didn't know something like that could happen so fast, but I'm pretty sure if someone asked him, August would say the same thing about me.

Kathleen decided to hire Caio to cater the wedding, even though flying him and his staff to Virginia for the weekend of the wedding and putting them all up in a hotel on top of the price of the catering itself added another thirty thousand dollars to the wedding budget. So tomorrow we're all heading back to New York in the Harkers' private plane for the tasting, which means I'm finally going to get to see August again.

It's almost midnight and I'm helping Mom clean up the tables of a beautiful harvest-themed wedding in an old barn on the outskirts of town, decorated in twinkle lights and kept warm with multiple space heaters, when my phone dings.

August: *I know we've got an early plane to catch, but are you up for another movie?*

Me: *Which one?*

August: *When Harry Met Sally.*

Me: *Ah, the classic to beat all classics. Good choice.*

August: *I thought so.*

Me: *I'll be home soon.*

August: *I'll be waiting.*

"What's got you smiling so big?" Mom asks, putting chairs up on the table next to me. She leans forward, studying my face. "And blushing?"

"Nothing."

I clean faster, my fingers whisking candles off centerpieces and folding tablecloths at inhuman speeds.

I can't wait to hear his voice again.

✳✳✳

A rainstorm hammers the roof as I lie in my pajamas on the couch, my phone cradled between my shoulder and my ear, listening to the gentle hush of August's breath over the receiver as Meg Ryan and Billy Crystal fall in love right before our eyes.

It hasn't escaped either of our notice how much like Harry and Sally we are, especially during the scenes where you see them watching movies together while talking on the phone to each other, their conversations peppered with a healthy balance of jokes and deep remarks.

August is the first one to voice it, even though it's been swirling in my mind for a while now.

"Wow," he says.

"What?"

"Do they remind you of anyone?"

A nervous laugh bubbles out of my throat. "A little."

August is quiet for a moment. Then: "Isla?"

"Yeah?"

"I'm glad I have a Sally in my life. Things would be pretty boring without you."

I refrain from reminding him that Sally ends up being Harry's soul mate, but just barely. Instead, I say, "That can't be true. You have Sophie."

A rush of breath huffs over my ear. It seems to be halfway between a scoff and a snort, but he doesn't say that I'm right or that I'm wrong, and somewhere deep inside my chest, something starts to ache.

"This is my favorite scene," I murmur sleepily into the phone as Harry and Sally stroll into the room housing the Temple of Dendur in the Metropolitan Museum of Art, their bodies silhouetted by a wall of windows overlooking Central Park. Harry asks Sally if she would like to go to the movies with him, but she tells him she can't because she has a date.

I sit up and pull my knees into my chest. "I don't know about you, but this is when I start wanting to rip my hair out, because it's so obvious they're meant to be together, but they just keep circling each other, and you wonder if they'll ever figure it out."

The line is quiet.

"August?"

"Have you ever been there?" he asks.

"Where?"

"The Met."

"No," I tell him. "But I've always wanted to go."

He hesitates.

"Maybe we can go together sometime."

"With Ryan and Sophie?"

"Maybe," he says. "Or maybe just you and me."

I shake my head, knowing that will never happen. "Sure. The next time we find ourselves with a couple hours to kill in New York City just the two of us, we'll go to the Met together."

"And reenact this scene?"

I laugh. "If you wish."

"I'm going to hold you to that, Riddle."

"I'm sure you will, Harker."

I'm also sure it will never happen. If anyone is going to the Met with August, it's going to be Sophie or some other girl who will catch his eye long after the wedding is over, and August and I have gone our separate ways. Maybe he'll find himself there years from now, staring at the Temple of Dendur, with a girlfriend or a wife—maybe he'll even have kids running around him by then—and he'll look up at the temple and think of this night, and of a girl who once kept him company on the phone when he couldn't sleep.

I hope when that time comes, he'll think of me fondly. If he isn't meant to be in my life forever, I at least want to be a good memory.

An hour later, the credits roll. I check the time on my phone. It's half past two o'clock in the morning.

"See you in a couple hours," August mumbles into the receiver.

"Just be ready to catch me if I slip in the rain," I joke.

"I'll always be ready to catch you," he replies, his words thick like he's speaking through a mouthful of honey.

The line goes quiet. I'm pretty sure he's fallen asleep.

"Promise?" I whisper, my heart hammering in my chest.

No response.

I'm about to pull the phone away from my ear, but then his voice, low and heavy with sleep, murmurs across the receiver.

"Promise."

15

✳✳✳

15

✳✳✳

I agonize over what to wear again, choosing a black cable-knit sweater dress, mocha-brown leggings, and black leather riding boots with brown leather accents—the perfect color palette for autumn in New York. I throw my hair up in a bun Audrey Hepburn would be proud of, bangs swept to the side, but the forecast from here to Manhattan calls for more rain, so I forego my usual Audrey-inspired eyeliner, choosing to highlight my mouth with a dark-brown matte lipstick instead. I finish the look with waterproof mascara and a vintage camel trench.

Mom freezes when she sees me. "Wow."

I tug on the wrist of my trench sleeve, suddenly self-conscious. "What?"

"You look amazing. I mean, you always look great, but today you just look so...grown up."

My smile is quick, like a shrug, but her words blossom in my heart. "Thanks."

"August will be impressed."

My cheeks warm.

"And it's casual enough not to upset the bride. Nicely done." Mom tucks her arm around mine as the Harker company car pulls into our driveway. "Let's go."

Just like before, August stands at the top of the plane steps when we get to the airport an hour later. This time, he's wearing a long brown coat that fits him perfectly, with a dark-gray sweater peeking out from underneath and a pair of European-cut jeans over leather ankle boots. He looks like a model who has literally just been ripped from the pages of *Vogue Paris*, and just like the first time I saw him standing at the top of those steps, I'm suddenly finding it very hard to breathe.

He helps Mom into the plane first, then takes my hand, his eyes twinkling.

"I can't have you falling down at the sight of me again," he teases.

I narrow my eyes at him. "Har har. Like that was the reason."

It was *totally* the reason.

He laughs and follows me into the cabin.

I half-expect Mrs. Harker to offer me another mimosa, but August places his hand on the small of my back, gently leading me past the table where Mom is already sitting with Mrs. Harker and Kathleen before she gets the chance. His hand guides me to the back corner where we sat before. Two coffee cups sit on the small window ledge between our chairs, a brown paper bag perched between them.

"What's this?" I ask.

He hands me a coffee. "Black, no sugar."

"You remembered."

"Hard to forget."

I take a sip. It's the perfect temperature, and the flavor

is bold but not bitter.

"And," he says as we take our seats, grabbing the brown paper bag, "the most delicious blueberry muffins you'll ever eat."

He pulls out a muffin the size of my hand. A golden-brown crumb topping dusted in sugar cubes glistens beneath the cabin lights, and blue spots on the liner where the berries burst and bubbled over stick like jam to my fingertips.

I groan at the sight of it. "Oh my gosh, you're perfect."

He freezes.

"I mean, they're perfect. *This*." I gesture at the coffee and muffins. "This is perfect."

He chuckles, shaking his head softly as he leans back in his seat. "I have to tell you, I've been looking forward to this all week."

I stop pulling the liner from the muffin. "You have?"

"I have *plans*."

"You always have plans."

"Yeah, but this is my best plan yet."

"Any hints?"

"Afraid not. You'll just have to wait and see."

I lean forward and whisper conspiratorially, "Are you going to cook something for the tasting and finally reveal your secret talent?"

His eyes widen. He glances back at his mom and sister, checking that they didn't hear me. "No," he says, taking a swig of his coffee. "That would be the *worst* plan."

"Some people on this plane disagree."

A muscle in his jaw ticks and the light in his eyes dims, and suddenly it's as if he's a thousand miles away from me.

The plane takes off, gliding into the sky. August watches the horizon as we break through the layer of gray clouds, swollen with rain, and into an orange-pink sunrise. But I don't watch the sunrise—I watch him. The fiery colors painting his face. The gravity in his gaze. The weight pulling him down like an undertow.

August Harker. I shake my head. *What am I going to do with you?*

✱✱✱

It's raining in Manhattan when we land, a light drizzle that plinks against the black umbrellas the Harkers loan Mom and me. Somehow, SoHo looks even more beautiful in the rain, with the underbelly of a swollen sky hanging low over us and squares of candy-yellow light pouring from every shop window reflected in the street's rain-slicked pavers, with the huge windows of aeliana shining the brightest of all.

Lily squeals as soon as she sees Kathleen and August and moves around the hostess station to check out Kathleen's gigantic ring once again ("It's so huge, I could die! How do you cart this thing around all day?"). I catch August's gaze flicking to the kitchen doors, his jaw clenching as he fights the desire that etches itself so clearly across his face. I suddenly wish I had an empty water bottle to hand to him and make a mental note to start keeping one in my bag, just in case. But then Lily is leading us to our table, and the tortured angles of his face soften. He smiles his casual smile, the one that people always think is real so long as they don't look too close.

I take his hand and give it a quick squeeze. I don't know if it's something a friend would do—I've never really been friends with a boy before—but I want him to know that someone here sees him. That someone here gets what he's going through and wishes they could make it better.

He squeezes my hand back. I'm vaguely aware of his lips silently forming the words *Thank you* as I sink into storm-gray eyes shaped with a gratitude so intense, it takes my breath away. There is nothing else around me, nothing else I see—just this boy who makes my stomach flip and my heart spiral every time he looks at me, who I am falling so madly in love with that I don't know how I'm ever going to say goodbye to him. And it physically hurts to be this close to him—to be stared at like this by him, like he's sinking into my eyes too and neither one of us wants to look away—and not be more to him than just a friend.

I thought I knew what falling in love would be like, but it's so much more terrifying and heart-wrenching and exhilarating than any romantic comedy could ever convey. And I think it would be worth it, feeling so out of control—palms sweating, knees shaking, heart breaking—if I knew we would have a happy ending, but I just don't see how our story can end in any way but bad.

And then Mrs. Harker asks August something about his upcoming meet schedule, and the moment ends. August answers her as he pulls out my chair for me. I don't miss the look Kathleen and Mrs. Harker share as I take my seat, nor the way my mom's eyes widen in a *told you so* kind of way, but August doesn't seem to notice.

Caio brings out a five-course meal, beginning with a salad course, followed by scallops and the most decadent butternut-squash risotto I've ever tasted. There's a fish course (halibut with a beurre blanc sauce) and then the main course—an herb-crusted rack of lamb with a garlic-cauliflower purée and pan-roasted vegetables. A mint sorbet to cleanse the palate finishes the meal, which will wrap up exactly thirty minutes before the cake is cut.

While everyone else is exclaiming over how great the food is, August holds each bite in his mouth and closes his eyes. I can practically see the gears of his mind working as he tries to detect each layer of flavor. His love for food is so obvious, I'm shocked his family hasn't noticed it.

"How do you do that?" I ask, catching him with his phone underneath the table, typing in ingredients and questions to ask Caio.

"Do what?"

"Figure out everything you're tasting."

He gives me his half smile, then takes my spoon and swirls it through my sorbet.

"Close your eyes," he tells me.

I look over at the others, but they're all so busy discussing the menu with Caio that none of them are paying any attention.

I close my eyes.

The cold, metallic curve of the spoon presses softly against my lips, pushing them apart. The even colder sorbet glides into my mouth, an explosion of mint on my tongue.

"Hold it against the roof of your mouth," August whispers, his breath warm on my neck. "Gently, so you don't get a brain freeze. Let it melt on your tongue. Do you taste the mint?"

I nod.

"Anything else?"

Underneath the mint, there's a layer of lemon and something else I can't quite place.

I tell him this, and I hear that small hitch of breath I know so well from the phone, the one that only happens when he's pleased.

"Champagne," he whispers, his voice rumbling over my skin.

My own breath catches.

"You can open your eyes now," he tells me.

I do.

His face is inches from mine, his gaze roaming from

my eyes to my lips and back again, and if we weren't at a table with our mothers in a crowded restaurant and if we weren't already taken—him by a real relationship and me by a fake one—I would almost swear he wants to kiss me.

"Now, then," he says, setting the spoon back down in the empty bowl. "Are you ready for your surprise?"

16

* * *

Our meal ends with a round of applause for Caio and with everyone in complete agreement that the menu is perfect for the reception. We all stand up from the table, gathering our coats from the backs of our chairs, ready to head to Rachel Lindberg's atelier for Kathleen's fitting, but August surprises me by turning to my mother and clearing his throat.

"Would you mind if I steal Isla away for a bit, Ms. Riddle?" he asks her. "There's something I'd like for her to see."

Mom gets that knowing smile again—seriously, could she be any more obvious?—and winks at us both. "Of course. Have fun."

August turns to me, his mischievous smile tugging at his lips. "Ready?"

I want to say yes—with every fiber of my being, I want to say yes—but I feel like I've been so distracted by this incredible boy that I've barely helped Mom with this wedding at all. Yes, I want to spend every moment I can with August before he walks out of my life forever, but what does it say about me that I'm so willing to blow off my mom to do that? I have responsibilities—things she's counting on me to do. I can't let her down.

"Hold on," I tell him. "I just have to check something."

I leave him at the table and take Mom aside.

"What's the matter, sweetheart?" she asks, her gaze sliding from me to August and back again. "Everything okay?"

"I don't have to go," I tell her. "I feel like I've been dropping the ball lately. Whatever August wants to show me, I can check out the next time I'm in New York." I say it like I come here all the time, but Mom and I both know that unless we start getting a lot of New York City brides wanting to work with us, this will probably be the last time either one of us is here for a while.

Mom glances at August, then takes my hands in hers and lowers her voice. "Sweetheart, I am so thankful that you're my partner and that we've built this business together, but you're trading the best parts of your teenage years for responsibilities that really shouldn't be on your shoulders yet. *Go.* Enjoy a rainy afternoon in New York City with a cute boy. I can handle one dress fitting by myself."

Tears prick my eyes. "Are you sure?"

"Positive."

I swallow. "Thanks, Mom."

She cups my cheek, and I'm surprised to see tears shining in her eyes too. "Just let me know when you get there safely."

"I will."

I turn back to August and give him a thumbs-up. His face is nothing short of radiant as he exhales, as if he were holding his breath waiting to see if I could go or not.

The rain plops against our umbrellas in big, fat bursts as August leads me outside. He hails a cab like a seasoned Manhattanite and asks the driver to take us to the Metropolitan Museum of Art as we scramble in.

My jaw drops. "The museum from *When Harry Met Sally*?"

He wriggles his eyebrows. "The very same one."

"So *that's* why you wanted to watch it last night."

August feigns innocence. "I don't know what you're talking about."

"Sure, you don't."

Sheets of water cascade from the sky, muddling the world outside our windows as the clouds seem to almost burst open above us. August narrows his eyes, trying to make out landmarks through the downpour, but he shakes his head, unable to see. Our taxi comes to a complete stop ten minutes later, where a construction zone has pushed all the traffic to the next street over from where we were supposed to turn.

"How far away are we?" August asks the driver.

"Two blocks," the driver responds.

August looks at me, then at the window again, then back at me. "Want to make a run for it?"

Run through a rainstorm with the cutest boy in the entire world?

I smile. "I thought you'd never ask."

August pays the driver and then takes my hand again as we duck out of the cab and onto the sidewalk. The rain is pounding the earth so hard that it splashes back up at us from the pavement, our umbrellas doing nothing to keep us dry as we race past Central Park, our feet slapping through leaf-strewn puddles, our laughter bouncing off passing buses and wind-stripped trees.

"These aren't even helping," August shouts as the wind scoops up our umbrellas, taking our arms with them.

"No, they're really not," I shout back.

"Here." August says, taking our umbrellas and handing them to another couple, who are holding soaking-wet magazines over their heads. "Maybe you'll have better luck with these."

The couple takes them and nods at us gratefully.

August pulls me forward and we run even faster without the weight of the umbrellas holding us back. Water cascades down our bodies as our breaths flow behind us in mingled white clouds.

"I can't believe you just did that," I shout over the rain's drumming cadence. "Won't your mom get mad?"

"Are you kidding?" he yells back. "We have at least a dozen more of those on the plane."

"Oh, right," I reply. "I keep forgetting you're rich."

"Does owning a dozen umbrellas make someone rich?"

"Mega rich."

"Damn," August says, tightening his hold on me. "Maybe I *should* look into that revolving closet."

I laugh until the tears in my eyes meld with the rain soaking my face, and August holds his side, saying it hurts too much to run and laugh this hard at the same time.

We make it to the steps of the Met, but I don't have time to look up and appreciate the view as we race up the stairs, through the doors, and into the museum. Water drips from our coats and onto the black weather mats lining the marble floors. The room is warm—thank God—but my clothes still feel like a layer of ice against my skin. I cross my arms over my chest, teeth chattering, knees knocking together. August looks at me, alarmed, then scans the room.

"Wait here," he says. "I'll be right back."

He darts into the gift shop. I pull my phone out and text Mom where we are, my hands shaking. She sends back a thumbs-up and an enthusiastic: *Have fun! :)*

August returns with two white beach towels bearing the Met's logo.

"Here." He quickly drapes one of the towels over his

shoulders and then wraps the other across my back, rubbing his hands up and down my arms to warm me up.

I glance at him through my lashes. "Thank you."

He hesitates, his hands slowing. "You're welcome."

We stare at each other, something so fragile passing between us, I don't even want to name it for fear I'll scare it away. And then August swallows and takes my hand, a gesture that is becoming more and more familiar—like our fingers were created to intertwine.

"Come on," he says, even though he didn't have to.

I would follow him anywhere.

August pays the admission fee and leads me through the Egyptian Art wing, past statuettes and Canopic jars and sarcophagi. He stops at a wooden chair from 1450 BC with claw feet and ivory accents.

"This is one of my favorite pieces," he tells me, one hand in his pocket, the other still wrapped around mine. "I look at this, and I try to imagine the person who made it, the people who've sat in it, and where it's been. It reminds me of how short our time here is—how we only exist for this brief moment, temporary travelers following the ones who came before us, with others coming up behind. I look at this chair, and it makes me want to live a life without regrets."

"Then why don't you?"

He looks down at my hand, as if suddenly realizing he never let it go. But he doesn't pull away. "That's easier said than done."

"We only get one life," I remind him as I stare at the chair, trying to see what he sees. "Do you really want to spend yours living a life someone else picked out for you?"

He opens his mouth. Closes it. Opens it again.

"Come on," he says finally. "This is just the tip of the iceberg."

He pulls me along behind him before I can say anything

else, switching the hand that is holding mine—right to
left—as we weave around a family inspecting a row of col-
orful pottery. And then he swings his arm around, pulling
me up so that I'm walking next to him. A minute later, there's
another group, another exchanging of hands as he pulls me,
once again, behind him. It's like a dance, how easily he ma-
neuvers our bodies through this space, as if we are one entity
swimming against the current.

We walk through a room with countless facsimile hiero-
glyphics depicting funerary processions as well as images
of the ancient Egyptians going about their daily lives. Every
face, every fragment of jewelry, every broken hair comb, every piece of art they made cries out to us. Their voices are
a current of energy that only grows louder, telling us how
short our lives are, reminding us that we are but a snatch of
vapor, a cloud of dust.

Make the most of your life, they seem to say. *Live each
and every moment.*

August was right. Everything in here is shouting at us,
warning us that life may seem like it lasts forever but it
doesn't, and suddenly these people who lived and loved
and died so long ago make me feel like I've been sleepwalk-
ing most of my life. Going through the motions. Waiting
for my life to really start.

August is the one who woke me up.

I don't know where this is heading. I don't know if he's
falling for me just as hard as I'm falling for him. I don't know
if holding my hand is like tethering himself to a harbor, a
place he never wants to leave, or if it's just something that
comes naturally to him, a born leader taking charge. I can't
read his mind, and I can't beg him to be anything more to
me than just a friend if he doesn't want to be. I can't shape
his life to my own in the same way his father tries to mold
him into the perfect replica of himself—because that would

be the ultimate betrayal, to try to manipulate August into something just because it's what I want.

No, I can't make August stay, but I can be here, fully present in the time we have together. I can glory in the wet tendrils of hair that have escaped my bun to lie across my neck. I can relish in the warmth of August's palm against mine. And I think to myself as we finally spill into the room of windows and light that I knew all along he was leading me to, I can live *this* day to the fullest.

No regrets.

✳ ✳ ✳

17

✳✳✳

We make our way to the wall of windows overlooking Central Park, the Temple of Dendur resting placidly behind us. The rain is still pummeling the earth, creating banks of mud in the grass and stripping red-and-purple leaves from the trees outside.

"I can't believe we're standing here," I whisper. "Right where they stood."

I glance over at August, amazed, but he isn't staring out the windows or reveling in the beautiful room we're standing in.

He's looking at me.

"I knew you'd like it," he says softly, and, for just a moment, his gaze is so intense it feels like my skin is on fire—like he's burning holes right through me. Like all he wants to do is push me up against the windows and kiss me until we melt into each other and become one person.

But I have to be wrong. He's with Sophie.

Sophie's not the one he calls late at night.
Sophie's not the one he shares his deepest secrets with.
When was the last time they were together anyway?
Maybe—

But then I remember his reaction at the conservatory, when it sounded like I was asking him out on a date and he sputtered as if he didn't know how to let me down easy, and that memory alone is enough to whip my gaze back to the windows, knowing I'm making up an entire romance between us that's only ever existed in my head.

"So." I clear my throat, trying to think of something to say. "Does everyone at your school know how much you love romantic comedies?"

August barks out a laugh and moves to stand beside me, hands in his pockets, gaze transfixed on the trees waving in the wind outside. "No, and they would harass me endlessly if they found out." His brows arch as he thinks about it. "I should tell them."

Now it's my turn to laugh. "Yeah, right."

"No, really. Maybe there are other guys who love them as much as I do but they're too afraid to speak up. I could start a rom-com revolution—tear down the walls of toxic masculinity and make it okay for men to feel."

"If anyone could do it, it's you. You are captain of the championship debate team, after all."

"Damn right I am." His eyes light up as if he's imagining what it would be like to start such a movement in his school, but then the light dims, and I watch his Adam's apple roll down his throat. "Only problem is I'm scared of what people think—always have been. It's kind of my downfall, really. This incessant need to be liked." He glances at the floor. "Pretty pathetic, huh?"

I look around the room. There's barely anyone else in here, just an older couple on the other side of the temple.

I inch closer. "It's not a bad thing to want to make people happy. It means you're a good person." Fear claws at my throat, knowing this may push him too far, but also knowing I may never get another chance. *No regrets.* "It only becomes a bad thing if you let it change who you are. Who—" I take a deep breath, then jump over the ledge, "—Who you're meant to be."

He rubs his hand across his mouth. "You're talking about cooking."

"I'm talking about the future Michelin-star chef standing right in front of me, if only he can find the courage within himself to chase after his dreams."

That muscle in his jaw ticks again. "You make it sound so easy."

I shake my head. "It won't be easy."

He turns his body toward mine. We're just as close as we were in the restaurant, only now our mothers aren't here.

I swallow. "But the best things in life rarely are."

His gaze moves from my eyes to my lips.

"Isla?"

I know I should back away—know I shouldn't let my true feelings for him bubble to the surface—but when I open my mouth, his name breaks across my tongue like a wave crashing against the rocks. "*August.*"

He slowly—hesitantly—places his hand under my chin, the tip of his thumb brushing my lower lip. I close my eyes. The scent of teakwood and orange blossoms and expensive leather envelops me. His hand moves up my jaw, fingers threading through my hair—

My phone *bings*, its echoing trill much too loud in this hushed room.

My eyes fly open.

August staggers back.

The look on his face—the obvious regret—breaks my

heart.

"Mom," I say, holding up the phone as I turn back toward the windows so he won't see me cry. I read the text. "They're ten minutes away."

He clears his throat. "We, uh, better head for the entrance, then."

I close my eyes, forcing them to stop burning. "Yeah. Okay."

He doesn't grab my hand this time, and I don't swerve around him in a dance that makes me feel more beautiful, more graceful, more ethereal than I've ever felt before.

Halfway to the entrance, August mumbles something I don't quite catch.

"What?" I ask.

"Your boyfriend," he says. "Does he like romantic comedies too?"

I take a deep breath. I don't feel like I have enough energy to keep up the lie. I open my mouth, ready to tell him there is no Ryan, but then I realize that would be even more humiliating than what almost just happened between us, so I shake my head and force out, "He's more of an action-movie kind of guy. You know, big explosions and unnecessarily long car chases? That sort of thing."

He snorts. "What could you possibly see in a guy like that?"

I know I should grit my teeth and not say anything back, but I'm just so tired of skirting around the giant supermodel elephant in the room—the one that *should* keep him from grabbing my hand at every opportunity and talking to me on the phone every night but that for some reason doesn't, and before I can stop myself, my eyes narrow and the words "What could you possibly see in such a self-centered girl?" come shooting out of my mouth.

He stops. "Excuse me?"

"Sophie." I spit out her name like it's poison on my tongue.

"And all of those stories she posts where she blatantly hits on every guy she comes into contact with."

His brow furrows. "You watch her stories?"

"Not lately, but I've seen enough to know that if you're really the kind of guy who wants to date a girl like that—a girl who surrounds herself with gyrating men just to make you jealous—then you can have her."

I turn on my heel and walk away, arms crossed, fingertips clinging to the edges of my rain-soaked towel. *Don't cry.*

Don't cry, don't cry, don't—

August's footsteps echo through the lobby as he races to catch up to me. "Isla, wait."

I turn back to him. "What?"

I say it louder than I meant to. A couple tourists stop and stare at us.

August runs his hands through his hair. "I don't know why I'm with Sophie, okay?"

I arch a brow. "Well...maybe you should figure it out."

"Yeah," he says, stuffing his hands in his pockets. "Maybe I should."

He looks like he wants to ask me something, but he can't quite bring himself to do it. I give him ten more seconds to muster up the courage, then huff out a breath.

"We should go," I say, my voice flat, betraying nothing. "We don't want to keep the plane waiting."

August follows me back out into the rain. He hails a cab, keeping a yardstick of distance between us, and then we're off to the airport, neither of us saying a word.

We don't talk as we head up the stairs to the plane, nor as we take our seats. I assume the silence will last the entire ride home, but once we're in the sky, August pulls something out of his bag and places it on the little table attached to my chair.

A tiny model of the Temple of Dendur.

"I bought it in the gift shop earlier. Before—" He stops, and I finish the thought for him. *Before our fight.* "To remember me by." He clears his throat. "When all of this is said and done."

I take the miniature temple and turn it over in my hands. "Thank you. I love it." And because I can't stand not talking to him anymore, I add, "I'm sorry for what I said about Sophie. I don't even know why I said it. I think—I think I just wanted you to know she's lucky. To have you, I mean." I hold his gaze. "Don't let her make you think otherwise."

His lips tilt into an almost-smile. "Ryan's lucky too, you know. To have you."

I give him a fake smile back.

And it feels like we're returning to the place where we were before—the friend zone—and even though it's not what I want, I'm thankful, because I'd rather have August think of me as a friend than as nothing at all.

18

✳✳✳

"Let me get this straight," Evelyn says, trees whizzing behind her as she power-walks to class. "He took you on the most romantic date I've ever heard of *and* almost kissed you, and you *still* think he's hung up on this Sophie girl?"

It's Monday morning, and she's hustling to class, while on the other side of the split screen, Savannah is standing in line at her favorite coffee shop, looking half-asleep after staying up all night studying. (She's been doing that a lot lately, and we haven't gotten too many words from her in recent phone calls other than "Huh?" and "What?" and "Need. Coffee.")

"I don't *think* he's hung up on her," I reply, the words coming out gross-sounding and weird from all the snot clogging up my nostrils. I grab the last tissue from the box that was full when Mom plopped it on my bed an hour ago and blow my nose. "I know he is."

Savannah moves up the line and orders a cappuccino,

then groggily murmurs into the phone, "Look, I know I'm not a love expert or anything, but this guy clearly likes you."

I roll my eyes. "If he *clearly* liked me," I reply, stuffing the used tissue into a plastic bag underneath my bedside table, "he'd have dumped Sophie by now and asked me out. But he hasn't, and he won't, and do you know why? Because Sophie is gorgeous and rich and semi-famous, and she's everything I'm not."

I half sob, half choke out the last words as a coughing fit squeezes my lungs. I grab the infrared thermometer from the pillow next to me and point it at my head.

99.3.

"But you said he almost kissed you," Evelyn points out. "He wouldn't do that if he wasn't into you."

"Yeah, but then he looked horrified after, like he didn't know what he was thinking." My eyes water, and I grab another tissue to wipe them. "He probably got all caught up in the *When Harry Met Sally*–ness of it all. We did watch the movie the night before we went, and we were standing right where they stood."

Evelyn stops outside the doors of a brick building and starts ticking points off on her fingers. "He watches movies with you every night by phone, he buys you coffee and replicas of ancient Egyptian temples, *and* he calls you beautiful. He. Is. In. To. You."

"He asked me what my type is so he could set me up with someone."

Savannah practically melts into a seat in the corner of the coffee shop, laying her head against the table as she waits for her coffee. "See?" she mumbles. "This is why I don't date. I get enough signals crossed in my life as it is."

Evelyn and I both stop what we're doing and immediately focus on her.

"What's going on, Vanna?" I ask her, worrying about

her dyslexia even though she swore the other day that it was fine. She just works so hard to beat it that, sometimes, when she's overworked or overstressed, her systems fail, and it gets worse.

"I don't want to talk about it," she grumbles. "Let's go back to deciphering silly boy code."

"At least you only have two more days until Thanksgiving break," I tell her. "Maybe you can get some sleep then."

She sighs into the polished woodgrain. "I can't."

"Why not?"

"I'm really behind on my schoolwork, and Mom...let's just say things aren't the best with her at the moment. It's better that I stay away."

"Is she having boyfriend trouble again?" I ask.

Her scalp moves up and down as she nods her face against the table.

"I'm so sorry, Vanna."

She shrugs. Things have always been touch and go with her mom, but it's been even worse the past few years, and Evelyn and I both know it bothers her more than she lets on.

"Yeah, I won't be making it home for Thanksgiving either," Evelyn says. "Beckett is taking me to meet his mom."

"Ev!" I shout. "That's huge!"

Evelyn blushes. "You think?"

"Flying you out of state to meet the mother?" Savannah mumbles, her face still pressed against the table. "Yeah, I'd say that's pretty big."

"I mean, we already knew Beckett was in it for the long haul, but still," I add.

Evelyn shrugs, but her smile is so bright, she could guide lost ships through the dark by the light of her teeth alone. "His mom's been doing really well too. She's been clean for six months now, and she's part of a support group at her local church. Beck really thinks this time might be different for her."

"That's incredible, Ev," I say.

Savannah puts both thumbs up.

Evelyn grins as she hitches the strap of her book satchel higher on her shoulder. "Anyway, enough about me. We need to help you figure this out. Go back to the beginning, when August flirted with you on the airplane steps."

I open my mouth to tell them, once again, how wrong they are, and immediately hack up a lung.

"On second thought," Savannah says, picking her head up. There's a pink mark on her forehead from the table, and her mascara is smudged under her eyes. "You sound terrible. Get some sleep."

"Yeah," Evelyn says. "You'll need your strength for watching another movie tonight with this guy who supposedly doesn't like you."

My entire body deflates as I sink down into the bed. "I want him to like me."

Evelyn softens. "We know you do."

We say goodbye, and I promise to rest—if by "resting", they mean binge-watching every Nora Ephron movie ever made—but then my phone *bings*.

A text from August.

I sit up.

August: *I need to talk to you. Will you be at the office tonight? Mom said you guys are going over the music for the reception.*

Me: *Mom will be there, but I won't. I'm sick.*

A minute passes. I wait for the three dots to appear, but they don't. I'm about to put my phone down when it rings.

August.

I try to clear my throat, but there's so much mucus that it's a losing battle, and my voice sounds like someone scraped my tonsils with a square of sandpaper when I answer. "Hello?"

"You sound terrible."

"Good morning to you too. Aren't you supposed to be in class?"

"I'm between classes at the moment. What's wrong?"

"I have a cold."

He curses under his breath. "This is my fault, isn't it?"

"What? No—"

"I should've never made you run in the rain like that."

"You ran the exact same distance, and you didn't get sick."

"Rich people don't get sick."

"Har har." My nose tickles. I squeeze my eyes shut to keep from sneezing in his ear.

"Should I tell Kathleen to reschedule so your mom can be with you tonight?"

The concern in his voice makes me snuggle into my mattress, wishing he was the one holding me instead. "Mom has back-to-back meetings, so she won't be home until ten at the earliest even if Kathleen does cancel, which she totally can't because we don't have time for that. Besides," I say, sniffling, "I don't need her to. I've got plenty of shows to binge and a few boxes of mac 'n' cheese in the pantry. I'll be fine."

My *fine* comes out with a hard *d* at the end. *Find.*

A rush of breath blows across the receiver. I can practically hear him shaking his head. "I'm coming over."

"What?"

"I'm coming over, and I'm making you soup." His voice is punctuated by the loud clang of a locker closing. "Any special requests?"

August Harker *cannot* see me all congested and red eyed and sweaty in old pajamas. "You can't. You'll get sick."

"I just told you," he replies. "Rich people don't get sick."

"August."

"Isla."

"I'm serious."

"So am I. I'm not going to let you be alone tonight." He hesitates. "Unless Ryan is coming over—"

"He isn't," I say—because he isn't a real person, but then I realize I should've said he is because that would've stopped August from coming.

"Great. I'll be there at five. Text me your address."

"But—"

"If you don't text it to me, I'll just walk down street after street shouting your name until I find you, but I'm begging you—don't make me do that. I really don't feel like looking like an ass in front of your entire hometown tonight."

"August—"

He hangs up before I can say another word.

I fall back against my pillows, too weak to do anything but whimper.

19

✳✳✳

After a full day of Netflix bingeing, I manage to gather enough energy for a shower and a spritz of gardenia perfume before pulling on a fresh pair of pajamas still warm from an extra tumble in the dryer, but I lose all steam the second I try to do anything with my hair, so I just let it air dry and throw it up into a messy bun. Then I pass out on the couch with my grandma's knitted blanket on top of me and my used tissue bag on the floor and wake three hours later to the sound of the doorbell ringing.

I blink, taking in the darkness pressing up against the windows. I check the time on my phone. Six o'clock.

The doorbell rings again. I wrap the blanket around my shoulders and stumble toward the door, whining as the pressure in my sinuses builds. I open the door, and of course August is standing there, looking perfect as always in his tailored coat over his sweats, his hair slightly messy from practice. He's carrying two brown-paper grocery bags with something green and leafy sticking out of the top of one of them.

"Sorry," he says. "I got here as fast as I could. Coach kept us late, and then there was traffic—"

He stops, his eyes raking over me as I shiver beneath the blanket. My eyes are giant pools that the shape of a blurry August is swimming in, and my nose is scraped raw from the number of times I've blown it.

August steps inside, setting the bags on the entryway table, and then he's rubbing his hands up and down my arms to warm me just as he did yesterday at the museum. "You're freezing. Do you have any more blankets?"

I tilt my head toward the family room. "In there."

He tries to guide me back to the couch, but I feel so weak and hungover from sleep, I can barely move. I start to tell him to just leave me in the entryway—I could bunch up the area rug to make a nice pillow—but he scoops me up into his arms before I can find the strength to open my mouth, carrying me without even the slightest hint of strain across the length of the family room. He lays me down gently on the couch, propping my head against the pillow I'd been using earlier. A basket of blankets sits next to the fireplace; he takes one from the top and drapes it over me, but my teeth are still chattering just as fast as those wind-up toys at the dollar store. He grabs another blanket and another, then puts his hand on my forehead. "You're burning up. Have you taken your temperature?"

I shake my head.

"Do you have a thermometer?"

I think about directing him to the forehead one currently lying on my bed, but then he'd see how messy my room is.

"Medicine cabinet," I murmur. "First floor bathroom."

My face feels like someone smashed it with a brick. I close my eyes and listen to his footsteps as he heads down the hall. He must find the bathroom because I hear the mirror swinging open next.

His footsteps head back my way.

"Open up," he tells me.

I do as he asks. He slides the thermometer under my tongue, then sits on the edge of the coffee table as he waits for it to beep.

"One hundred and two," he says after it's gone off. "Have you taken any medicine?"

I shake my head again.

He takes the thermometer back to the bathroom. I hear the faucet running, and then the cap being replaced on the thermometer and the mirror gently closing.

August returns carrying a brand-new, plastic-wrapped package of liquid cold medicine. He rips off the plastic, checks the dosage, and then pours some into the tiny measuring cup for me.

"Drink."

I narrow my eyes. "It's purple."

"Some people would call that grape."

"I prefer cherry."

He smirks. "I'll remember that next time."

I take the cup from his hands and down it in one gulp.

August takes the cup from me, pushing my hair off my face. "You just lie here. Soup will be ready in thirty minutes."

I listen to his footsteps heading toward the kitchen and then to the opening and closing of cupboards, the sliding of a pot onto the stove, the gentle crack of a cutting board being set on the counter. I can hear him washing and dicing the vegetables, doing that lightning-quick chopping thing I saw him do at the restaurant.

I must fall asleep again because it seems like only a minute passes before August is standing in front of me, holding out a bowl of soup wrapped in a towel to protect my hands from the heat seeping through the bottom.

I try to sit up, but the entire world swims across my eyes. August sets the bowl on the coffee table and helps me, propping up some pillows on my left side before sitting on my right to buffet that side as well. Then he hands me the soup and puts his arm around the back of the couch. His body is so warm, and I am so cold that I don't even hesitate to cuddle into him, like a cat curling up to a radiator.

"That feels nice," I tell him, my voice coming out smoother than before. The medicine has made me less congested, but it's also making me feel kind of funny, like my head could float right off my body. He stiffens, but I'm too woozy to care if I'm crossing the dreaded "friend line" again. He can just deal with it if I am.

"Let's see what there is to watch," he chokes out, grabbing the remote and coughing into his hand.

"Careful," I tell him, slurring my words slightly. "I was using that earlier. You're holding a portable germ factory."

"Not to worry," he says, gesturing to the side table, where he's laid out a fresh box of tissues along with a bottle of hand sanitizer and a packet of sanitizing wipes. "I came prepared."

"I thought rich people don't get sick."

"That's preposterous. Who told you that? We're rich, not superhuman."

I glare at him and open my mouth to protest, but he just shakes his head.

"Eat your soup."

"What are these little round things?" I ask.

"Lentils. They're full of zinc—good for the common cold and other ailments. There's also garlic, ginger, shallots, and turmeric, all supporters of the immune system. And chicken because, well, chicken is delicious."

I lean forward and try a spoonful while August surfs through our streaming apps, making a list of possible movie choices.

"This is amazing," I say, mouth-breathing all over the soup.

August smiles. "I'm glad you like it."

"I'm serious," I say, meeting his gaze. "Go to culinary school. Become a chef. You already cook like one."

He rolls his eyes. "This again."

"Yes. *This* again. And it will be 'this again' every day of my life until you stop being such a blockhead and do what God created you to do."

He stares down at the remote in his hand.

"You know..." His brow furrows. "No one's ever talked about a career like that to me, like I have this specific calling that only I can do. I've always been told that jobs are a means to an end, with the 'end' being at least seven figures in the bank account, a nice house in a gated community, a couple vacation homes, a yacht or two." He grits his teeth. "It can be hard to fight that kind of thinking when it's been programmed into you your entire life."

"But you're already fighting it."

"What do you mean?"

"Being born into a wealthy family with unlimited opportunities at your disposal could make you a real jerk, but you're not."

"You haven't seen how I behave when there's only one piece of sushi left on the table." He wriggles his eyebrows. "I'm ruthless."

"I'm serious," I say, holding his gaze. "You once told me I don't know how beautiful I am. Well...you don't know how amazing you are, and you let people walk all over you because of it."

"You mean my dad and Sophie?"

I shrug.

He clears his throat, but his phone beeps before he can

say anything. He checks the text, muttering something under his breath. "Speaking of Sophie," he says, stuffing the phone back into his pocket. "She's pissed I'm blowing her off again."

Some small part of me knows I should tread lightly—especially after our fight at the Met—but it's like the medicine has torn out whatever semblance of a filter I had left because next thing I know, I'm saying, "You've been doing that a lot lately."

"Yeah. I guess."

"Have you figured out why you're with her yet?"

He takes a deep breath, thinking. Then, hesitantly: "She's my father's choice."

"*Eww.*"

He laughs. "Not like that. She just...completes the picture, you know? Head cheerleader, honor student, comes from the right sort of family—"

"Gorgeous?"

He meets my gaze, then glances back down at the remote. "I've seen prettier."

I stir the spoon around the bowl, my heart thumping. "That still doesn't answer my question."

He swallows. "I guess I'm still trying to figure it out."

"Well, maybe you should try a little harder."

"Yeah," he says, echoing our parting words at the Met. "Maybe I should."

A beat passes.

Neither of us says a word.

August reaches for me, and for a second, I think he's going to grab my chin again, just like he did at the Met. My brain starts freaking out, worried our first kiss will be full of snot and germs and the coughing fit that's sure to attack at any moment, and then I'll forever be *that girl* who hacked up a lung into his mouth, and I don't know if I could survive the humiliation of it. But he rests his hand against my forehead instead and I realize he's just taking my temperature again.

"You seem a little cooler," he says. "The medicine must be working."

I lean into the comfort of his palm and whimper slightly when he pulls it away.

I finish the soup while we debate movie titles. We settle on Nancy Meyers's *Father of the Bride* because it feels appropriate given the fact that the wedding is only a few weeks away. August gets the movie all cued up, then takes my bowl into the kitchen, washing it out in the sink.

He comes back with the other grocery bag.

"Ready for your surprise?" he asks.

"That's the second time you've asked me that in two days."

He shrugs. "I like surprises."

He tips the bag so I can see the contents. It's full to the brim with movie theater candy. Milk Duds and Sno-Caps and Sour Patch Kids. Reese's Pieces and M&Ms and Red Vines.

"I didn't know which kind you liked," he says, "so I grabbed everything they had."

"Wow," I say, marveling at the assortment of brightly colored boxes. "Thank you."

"I figured our first time watching a movie together in person should come with the real thing. I could make popcorn too, if you want?"

I shake my head and pat the couch, gesturing for him to sit back down. "No, the soup was plenty. Thank you."

I take the Sour Patch Kids. He takes the Red Vines.

August presses Play, and the movie begins with its iconic Alan Silvestri theme playing over a background of golden champagne bubbles. August pats his chest and, after just a moment's hesitation, I lay my head in the crook between his collarbone and his shoulder, breathing in that scent that I love so much. Teakwood and orange blossoms and expensive leather now mixed with a touch of sweat from running. I relish in the softness of his shirt and the hardness of his muscles underneath. At the way his body goes rigid as I snuggle against him, looking to seep every last ounce of warmth from his skin.

"You know, for all of my Nora Ephron talk," I tell him, my medicine-laced voice slurring the words together, "I have to admit that this movie is the one that made me want to be a wedding planner, even before Mom got into it."

"What's your favorite thing about weddings?" he asks, his body relaxing slightly, as if he's slowly giving himself permission to ease into the couch.

"My favorite part is watching how the love a bride and groom share doesn't just impact the two of them—it brings two completely different families together to make a new one. And I love the wedding toasts, when people talk about who the bride and groom were before they knew each other, who they are when they're together, and all of the hope everyone has for them for the future. It's a time to celebrate and a time to remember and a time to hope. A completely new chapter for everyone involved."

"Yeah," August says. He gently, hesitantly, brushes a lock of hair behind my ear. "I'm starting to get that."

The blanket shifts, exposing the small of my back. His fingertips accidentally graze my skin as he moves to right it, and his muscles tighten once again.

I don't move.

He doesn't either.

Then his thumb starts making small, questioning circles against my lower back, and even though our eyes are glued to the TV, I know neither one of us is focused on anything but the feeling of his skin against mine.

I glance up at him, at the hard line of his jaw as he clenches his teeth, the slight flaring of his nostrils as his breathing grows shallow. I can feel his heartbeat picking up through his shirt. He shifts down more so that he's lying across the couch, his feet tangled up in mine, with only the top of his chest and head propped up. I'm lying on my side, in the seam of the couch. I wiggle deeper into his warmth and sigh as his heat chases away the chill.

He moves his hand up to my hair again. This time his nails lightly scratch my scalp as he runs my hair through his fingers.

It feels like the most natural thing in the world for my body to be tangled up in his.

I don't know when I fall asleep. One second George Banks is meeting Franck (the wedding planner to beat all wedding planners), and the next second the credits are rolling and I'm all wrapped up in the blankets, but my warmth is gone.

August isn't here.

I blink away the dregs of sleep and the fuzziness of the medication. It takes me a second to realize the water in the kitchen sink is running again. There's the clank of pots hitting one another, the sound of the dish soap bottle being squeezed, and the light *hush-hush* of a scrub pad against ceramic. The dishwasher clicks closed and the buttons beep as August starts it up.

He walks back into the family room, wiping soap from his forearms with a dish towel. He throws the towel over his shoulder and squats down next to me, checking my temperature again. "How are you feeling?"

"Tired," I mumble.

"It's almost ten. Your mom should be home soon. Do you want me to stay until she gets here?"

No, I want you to stay forever.

"I'll be okay," I tell him, my heart breaking a little as I do. "Besides, we don't want anyone to think this was anything more than what it was."

His lips twitch. "And what was it?"

"You were just helping out a friend," I say, closing my eyes.

He doesn't answer.

"Right?" I ask, peeking up at him through my lashes.

"A friend." He swallows. "Right."

He pulls the blanket up to my shoulders, tucking it around me. He hesitates. And then he slowly, *gently*, presses his lips against my brow. "Good night, Isla Riddle."

My throat goes dry.

"Good night, August Harker."

20

***

I'm still sick on Thanksgiving, so Mom makes turkey-rice soup instead of going all out with our traditional Thanksgiving dinner. My grandma wanted to come, but we tell her to stay away—she doesn't need to get what I have. We promise to come to her house for Christmas instead. In fact, Mom doesn't have a wedding booked for the following Saturday—the day before New Year's Eve—which is a strange aberration for us, so she talks about staying the entire week and taking our first true vacation in over a year.

I tell August all of this through text. He asks to hear every detail of the trip we're planning, practically begging me to keep his mind off of the mind-numbingly dull Thanksgiving he's having at the country club, with his dad schmoozing every potential client in sight and his mom outright flirting with his father's colleagues to try to make him jealous (I refrain from asking him if it reminds him of anyone, but just barely). Kathleen and her husband-to-be are all wrapped

up in each other—rightfully so—and August says he's just
sitting alone at their table, looking like the saddest puppy
in the litterbox.

Me: *Where's Sophie?*

August: *Skiing in Vermont with her family.*

The three dots appear and disappear. Appear and disappear. Like a dance.

I can't take my eyes away.

Finally, his text comes through.

August: *Where's Ryan?*

Me: *With his family. I didn't want to get him sick.*

The lie stings. The weight of it is becoming more
than I can bear, but I also like the confidence Fake Ryan
gives me—the image it projects that I'm not just waiting
around for August to make a move that I'm not even sure
he wants to make.

August: *How are things going with him?*

Me: *How are things going with Sophie?*

I hate that I sound like a jealous girlfriend when we aren't
even dating, but there's something building between us. The
night he spent here proved it. Friends don't draw circles on
their friends' backs as if memorizing the shape and pattern
of their spines. They don't kiss each other's foreheads, or
hold you like you're the most fragile thing in the world and
they're terrified of breaking you. But I also know that he's
still with her, and I can't deny that every time we've gotten
close to anything more happening between us, he's backed
off, so whatever it is he feels for me, it's not enough to change
anything between us.

August doesn't answer my question.

I don't answer his either.

A half hour later, Mom and I are watching *Christmas
Vacation* in the family room while decorating our Christmas tree—a Thanksgiving tradition to officially welcome

the Christmas season—when he texts again.

August: *Dad is making ME schmooze now. SEND HELP.*

Me: *Just tell them you think they're all crooks and they should be in prison.*

August: *Haha, Dad would have a fit.*

August: *I love it.*

A beat passes.

August: *I wish you were here.*

I hesitate because admitting it feels like giving away too big a piece of myself, something I can never get back once it's out there, but then my fingers are typing, and I hit Send before I can stop myself.

Me: *I wish you were here too.*

August: *:)*

August: *What are you doing right now?*

Me: *Watching Christmas Vacation.*

August: *Can I watch it with you?*

Me: *How are you going to do that?*

August: *Text it to me. Tell me what's happening.*

So I do. I text him summaries of each scene, my fingers flying over the phone as I text him all the lines that make me smile, and he texts lines back, ones he's clearly memorized.

Mom smirks as she watches me. "August?"

I nod.

"Tell him I said hi."

By the end of the movie, Mom and I are sending him reels of us reenacting the squirrel-jumping-out-of-the tree scene, and August is sending back hysterically laughing GIFs in response, and even without him here, August has somehow made this the best Thanksgiving of my life.

21

✳✳✳

I'm well enough by Sunday to go with Mom to the grooms-men's final tux fittings. In truth, I would've gone even if I weren't feeling better. It's been too long since I've seen August, and I feel like half of my heart has been missing for the past week without him next to me, especially now that we're running out of time. The wedding is two weeks away, and then after that...what? Will we keep talking even though we live an hour away? Will I be the eternal friend, watching from the sidelines as he marries Sophie and becomes every-thing he hates? Or will we drift apart? Will he become the boy I measure every future relationship against? And what will I be to him? The girl who once kept him company when he couldn't sleep?

The tux shop is in Richmond. Mom and I grab a Pop-Tart each and leave at eight for the hour-long drive. We go through the wedding checklist for the thousandth time, checking and rechecking that everything is on schedule:

vendors are confirmed; flower delivery is on track; bridesmaids all have their dresses; and, most importantly, all the money spent has been accounted for, as well as the hours spent pulling everything together. It's our usual routine, but it's different this time because this is our first big-budget wedding. Everything has to go off without a hitch. And still, even with the stakes so high, my mind keeps drifting back to skyscraper eyes and circles on skin and that slow, easy smile that makes my whole body sing, and I have to refocus back on Mom, on the checklist, on my own uneven breaths shaking out of my body just to keep myself from falling into despair at the knowledge that it's almost over. That August Harker and his crinkling water bottles and his treasure trove of smiles will soon be nothing but a haunted memory of a boy who carries my heart around in his hands and doesn't even know it.

We're fifteen minutes late due to unexpected traffic. Three of the groomsmen are already in their tuxes, the shop's tailor marking measurements on the fabric in chalk while Kathleen worries over the fit. Mom hurries over to remind the tailor that we're going for the more form-fitting European look. The two other groomsmen I don't know—fraternity brothers of the groom's—are off to the side, rearranging the mannequins to make it look like they're doing something extremely inappropriate with a pair of suspenders, and Kathleen's fiancé is sitting on a leather couch, watching *SportsCenter*. I roll my eyes at them and focus on August, who's standing in the middle of the store, one hand in his pocket, the other holding his tux bag over his shoulder.

"Hey," he says. "Just in time for the show."

"I wouldn't miss it."

We both move awkwardly, as if we aren't sure if we should go in for a hug or not. Things are different since the night he came over, and neither one of us knows how to act. I wonder if he regrets it, if he's kicking himself for crossing the friend line that he seems so determined to keep.

August clears his throat. "I should hit the changing room while it's free."

I glance at the frat boys, now watching a replay on TV of a college football tackle that leveled a guy yesterday and landed him in the hospital. They keep stopping and rewinding it and making terrible faces every time the helmets smack.

"I think Dumb and Dumber will keep for a while," I tell him.

August winces. "I don't know how I'm going to spend the entire wedding day with those guys."

"Earbuds?"

"For starters." He shakes his head. "I'll be out in a minute."

He disappears into the changing room. I try really hard not to think about the fact that August Harker is undressing himself just a few feet away from me and the only thing separating us is a beige curtain.

Think of something else. *Anything* else.

Puppies. Grandma. Kites. The beach.

August at the beach. August taking his shirt off at the beach—

UGH. NO.

I force the image away and try again.

Christmas. Santa. Reindeer. Snow.

A hot tub in the snow. August in the hot tub in the snow—

"Isla?"

"Nothing!" I whirl around. "I didn't say anything."

Please God, don't let me have said anything.

August peeks at me through the curtain. "Could you get someone to help me? I can't get the tie to lay right."

"I can help with that."

His brow arches. "You know how to knot a tie?"

"Two years working in the wedding industry, remember?

I can do a Windsor, a four-in-hand, and a trinity with my eyes closed."

"Wow." He blinks. "I can't even manage a simple knot most days."

"Here," I say, walking into the dressing room without thinking. "Let me see."

Kathleen wants an Eldredge knot, which is the most difficult to pull off, but I've had plenty of practice. Still, I didn't think about the fact that I've never knotted a tie on a boy I've liked before, let alone a boy I'm falling head over heels in love with. His chin is barely an inch from my forehead as my hands maneuver the tie around his collar. I hope he can't tell how much they're shaking.

Wait.

Is it my imagination, or did August just move closer?

There's only a small gap of the curtain open, but when the frat boys start filming a video of themselves dancing in their tuxes, August swipes it closed the rest of the way.

"Sorry," he says. "I just don't feel like being in the background of whatever atrocity they're committing."

I smirk. "Good thinking."

My hands move deftly over the silk, looping it around and through and back again. My fingertips graze August's neck.

He closes his eyes.

I'm making the second-to-final loop when August's hand catches mine, holding it steady against his collarbone.

"Isla."

I'm mesmerized by his lips—by the shape they make as he stares down at me, by the rush of breath escaping them, by the fact that they aren't quirked up in some ghost of a smile, and by the way that they're moving steadily closer toward mine. And when they do meet, when his mouth locks against mine, they fit perfectly, as if our lips were made to do this.

My entire body goes weak. I practically fall against him, but his arms are already wrapping around me, steadying me, holding me tight as he deepens the kiss. My hands knot behind his back, pulling him closer. That's all I can think about, all I want—to be as close as possible to him.

He's clawing at my back and my fingers are in his hair, and there's no space for thought, for logic, for anything but hitches of captured breath and bodies pressed tight in a small changing room. He tastes like coffee and peppermint, and I know in this moment that I could spend days kissing him and not take a single break. It is everything I imagined it would be and so much more.

Much, *much* too soon, he tears his lips away from mine. I could cry at the feeling of him pulling away from me, except for the fact that it looks like it is the last thing he wants to do.

He presses his forehead against mine. His eyes are closed, his breathing rough. His hands lock at the small of my back, and that smile that I love so much, traces his swollen lips.

"I've wanted to do that since the moment I met you." His words shake as he tries to catch his breath. "I'm breaking up with Sophie tomorrow, at school. I would've done it sooner, but I wanted to do it in person, and she's been gone since Tuesday. Really, I should have done it sooner than that."

"Why didn't you?" I ask, my words barely above a whisper.

"At first it was out of loyalty. I'd been with her for almost a year, and I'm not one to break commitments easily. I'm also ashamed to admit that part of me was afraid to choose something for myself. To *love* something for myself. But you, Isla Riddle..." His eyes bore into mine. "I would walk through fire for you."

A strangled sob of relief escapes my lips as I look up at the ceiling, tears welling in my eyes. "I can't tell you happy it makes me to hear you say that."

"Does it really?" He takes another shaky breath. "When

you told me you had a boyfriend, I backed off, figuring you didn't want to be anything other than friends. But every time we were together, I could have sworn you felt it too, this energy between us. The way the air crackles every time you walk into a room. You make my head spin."

"But the conservatory..." I shake my head. "When I mentioned us going out to get cake together, you looked like I'd just asked you to step in front of a firing squad."

"I was ashamed at how badly I wanted to go with you. I was torn over how strong my feelings for you had become, knowing it was wrong for me to be dating Sophie while falling in love with you. Because that's what's been happening, Isla. Every single second of every single day. And I know you have a boyfriend, and you probably don't think of me in the same way, but—"

"I don't."

His entire body tenses.

"I mean, I *do*. Feel the same way about you." I take a deep breath. "I don't have a boyfriend."

"You and Ryan broke up?"

I swallow. "There never was a Ryan. I made him up."

"Why?"

"Because of the conservatory. When you looked at me like that, I thought you were horrified that I would even suggest something remotely close to a date. I made Ryan up to save face. Not very original, I know. It kind of tops the list of romantic-comedy screwups. But I was falling so desperately in love with you, and you were still with her, and I thought you only wanted to be my friend. I swear I never lie about anything, but I just couldn't handle the idea that I was falling for someone who could never think of me in the same way."

He doesn't respond.

"Are you mad?" I ask, my blood thumping in my ears.

"No. I'm not mad." His lips break apart into that glowing, heart-stopping, brighter-than-a-million-suns smile. "I'm *ecstatic*."

He scoops me up and spins me around, the bottoms of my shoes swishing against the curtain. I hold on tight to his neck, both of us laughing.

"Be my girlfriend, please," he says, setting me down. "Put up with my ridiculous fears and my embarrassing lack of a revolving closet. Be with me, every second of every day. I'll drive down and spend every day after practice with you if your mom will let me, and on the weekends, we'll go wherever you want to go. Richmond. New York. Paris. You pick." He rests his brow against mine again and closes his eyes. "Just be with me. Please."

My heart is so full, it feels like it could burst. I'm cry-laughing as he holds me. I didn't know it was possible to be this happy.

"I will," I tell him. "*After* you break up with Sophie."

He nods. "You understand why I want to do it in person, don't you?"

"The impatient part of my brain says no, but yes, I do. But do it first thing, okay? I want to be able to call you my boyfriend by lunchtime tomorrow."

He grins. "Now that's a promise I can keep."

He kisses me again, and I fall apart, bursting into the air like the birth of a star.

God, how I love this boy.

22

* * *

We spend the entire day with Mrs. Harker and Kathleen, going from the tux fitting to the opulent Jefferson Hotel for the final bridal fitting. We meet with the seamstress, who flew in from Rachel Lindberg's atelier in New York this morning. Kathleen's fiancé stays behind so as not to see the dress before the wedding, choosing to go to an NFL party with his groomsmen instead. Mom, Mrs. Harker, August, and I all wait in the sitting room of the seamstress's suite while Kathleen changes into her dress, our jaws dropping the moment the doors to the bedroom open and Kathleen steps out.

She looks like a blonde Kate Middleton, with delicate, embroidered lace sleeves and a body-hugging bodice that flares out in the trumpet style at the bottom. Her hair, which she curled this morning, is sideswept with a stunning diamond-and-pearl encrusted comb, a gossamer floor-length veil wafting behind her. Mom, Mrs. Harker, and I jump up and immediately start exclaiming over how gorgeous she looks, but when I glance back at August, he's still sitting on the couch, his jaw strung in a tight line. At first, I think he's angry about something, but then I notice the light reflected in his eyes, the tears he's trying so hard not to shed.

Kathleen crosses to him, pulling him into a long, wordless hug.

"I'm going to miss you, little brother," she tells him.

"Right back at you, big sister," August replies. Then, with a grin: "You don't have to marry him, you know."

Kathleen chucks him on the chin.

After the fitting, Kathleen leaves to meet up with her fiancé, but Mrs. Harker invites Mom and me back to the house for dinner. Mrs. Harker rides with Mom to go over some final decisions needed by the end of the day.

I ride with August.

It's only a little after four, but the sun is already setting. August's headlights turn on automatically in response to the growing darkness surrounding us as he pulls out of the hotel parking lot and onto the freeway. I watch his hands, mesmerized, as they move effortlessly over the steering wheel.

My boyfriend.

After tomorrow morning, August Harker will be my boyfriend.

We've spent the entire day together. Even after August's mom told him he wasn't needed anymore, he went everywhere with us. He was careful to only touch me when neither of our moms were looking, but he still found ways to make my breath catch even when he wasn't touching me—his breath tickling my neck as he whispered in my ear how much he adores me; his eyes boring into mine, looking at me with the same hunger and intensity that shaped his eyes at the Met, when I thought he was going to push me up against the windows and kiss me until we melded into one breath, one soul, one being.

My heart races now just thinking about it.

"Are you ready for this?" August asks as he pulls off the freeway.

"As ready as I'll ever be."

August's family lives in an affluent, gated community just outside of Richmond surrounded by acres and acres of woods. The bare trees claw the indigo sky as we pull through the first set of gates and up a long, curving road. Every house we pass is bigger than the one before it as we head deeper into the woods, and each one looks like it's trying to outdo the other in some sort of Christmas decorating competition. I marvel at flashing lights synchronized to Trans-Siberian Orchestra music and giant plastic snowmen waving at each other from opposite yards. I try to imagine what it must have been like for August to grow up here, in this neighborhood where so much wealth has been accumulated, and I can't help but wonder: Are these people happier because of it, or are they stuck in jobs that pay the mortgage but that make them a shell of the people they used to be, like August's dad?

"More money won't make you happy, Chris," Mom shouted at Dad after he told her he was leaving us to become a Hollywood agent. "You could accumulate all of the wealth in the world, but if you don't learn how to be content with what you have, it will never be enough."

It's probably not fair to lump in all these people with August's dad. I bet a lot of them would know how to be just as happy with little as they are with much—because that's what it's really about, isn't it? Cherishing the things that bring us true happiness?

Take this car. I can't even begin to imagine how much it's worth—it's all sleek lines and high-tech screens and seats that hug every curve of a person's body—but the car is not what makes this moment special. I would be just as happy riding on a cramped bus next to August, his arm pressed against my arm, our heads bowed, sharing whispered jokes and hushed laughter and crinkling eyes.

These houses are impressive, and there's a small part of me that grows jealous as we pass them by and I wonder what it would be like to live in one, but my mother's words echo in my head, and I remind myself that's all they are: houses. Places to live. They don't bring someone true joy on their own.

I slide my eyes to August, remembering him in the kitchen at aeliana, how free he was there, how natural as he slid into the rhythms and movements of shaping food that looked like art and tasted like heaven, and I realize that, for some people, these homes are full of life and laughter and love, but for others, these homes are nothing more than beautiful cages, trapping them in a life of expectations they could never meet.

Finally, August pulls into a driveway at the end of the road. There's a gate here too. August keys in a code to open it. The gate swings to the side, letting us through before closing behind us.

There are two more curves in the long drive, and then the trees open up, revealing a three-story contemporary mansion built of black iron and seamless glass. There are two balconies, one off the second floor and one off the third, also outlined in black, and a six-car garage beneath them. It's hard to tell in the dark, with the dazzling yellow Christmas lights lining the house and curling around the topiaries, creating a soft, golden glow over everything, but I'm pretty sure I also spot a pool, a tennis court, and a helipad on the rolling green lawn stretching out behind the house before the car wends around the circle at the end of the drive.

August parks next to Mom's car. My mouth drops as my gaze lands on the stone staircase leading to the front door, where water cascades down either side in twin waterfalls, backlit by golden underwater lights.

August opens my door for me. I step out, my shoes crunching gravel, my eyes wide as I take everything in.

"You lied," I tell him. "You *are* revolving-closet rich."

"Yeah, but..." August sighs as he looks up at the house. "It's not all it's cracked up to be."

I reach for his hand, threading my fingers through his own. "I know."

He turns to me, his lips twitching into that shrug-smile he gets whenever he's acknowledging something painful but doesn't want to give into it.

He squeezes my hand. "Ready?"

"As ready as I'll ever be."

We start up the steps, the waterfalls burbling on either side of us.

"This is beautiful," I tell him.

He nods. "It's the only thing I like about this house. Well, this and the pools."

"Pools?" I ask. "As in plural?"

He blushes.

I shake my head. "How you don't have a revolving closet is beyond me."

He laughs just as the front door creaks open ahead of us. We both glance up.

"Sophie," August blurts.

He drops my hand.

I tell myself it's just because he hasn't broken up with her yet, but the pain of his hand leaving mine is like a dagger slicing open my palm.

Sophie, oblivious, cascades down the steps as if she were a water nymph rising from the falls, all graceful lines and billowing, bell-shaped sleeves on a nearly see-through white linen dress. Her delicate, strappy heels look like they probably cost more than my car, and her skin is glowing with expertly applied bronzer and highlighter, making me feel like a troll who accidentally stumbled into this paradise by mistake.

She wraps her arms around August's neck, kissing him and making a *hmm* noise in the back of her throat.

I look away.

August wrenches himself out of her grasp. "What are you doing here?"

"Your mom invited me." She arches a brow and digs her pointer finger into his sternum. "I called her phone looking for you since you don't answer your texts anymore, and she said you would be home in time for dinner. We got home earlier than we expected, so Dad dropped me off."

August grits his teeth. "Sophie. We need to talk."

She cuts her mascara-rimmed eyes to me. "Hi, I'm Sophie," she says, cocking her head to one side as if I'm the cutest little non-threat she's ever seen. "Have we met?"

"Not officially," I reply. "I'm one of Kathleen's wedding coordinators."

August puts his hand on the small of my back.

I close my eyes. He's still here. Still with me.

"This is Isla," he says. "I've told you about her."

He has?

She narrows her eyes at August's palm against my spine. I can see her mind putting it together—August saying they need to talk; his hand on my back; the way his stance has grown almost protective, as if shielding me from her.

"Whatever," Sophie says, as if she couldn't be bothered to remember me. She crosses her arms. "Can we talk later? I'm starving, and Armando made his famous shrimp scampi. Armando's their cook," Sophie adds, turning to me. "Do you eat carbs?"

My brow furrows. "Um...yes?"

"Ugh, lucky. I don't. Haven't had a single carb in two years. Armando's kind enough to put the shrimp in a salad for me instead. But beauty is pain, right?" She says this last part while raking her eyes up and down my body as if she could tell I'm a carb-eating machine from a mile away.

"Sophie—" August steps forward, a note of warning in his voice, but she's already twirling back toward the open front door.

August grits his teeth as she disappears inside.

I glance uncertainly at the open door. "Maybe my mom and I should go. Grab a pizza or something—"

He turns to me, taking both of my hands in his. "No, please. Stay." Desperation claws at his voice. "I've been waiting all week to see you."

I bite my lip.

"I swear." He raises my hands to his mouth, brushing his lips across my knuckles. "I'm walking through that door, and I'm breaking up with her. I'll take her to the library so no one will hear, and then I'll drive her home and be back in five minutes flat." He draws me close, pushing the strands of my hair behind my ears and resting his head on top of mine. "You are all that I've ever wanted, Isla. Please don't go just because I was a total moron and didn't break up with her sooner."

I swallow. "Okay."

August leads me through the front door—made from such a thick slab of ebony that it thuds closed like a thunderclap behind us—and into the main room.

The entire first floor is open concept, the same ebony wood stretching across the floor in wide planks. To the right is the kitchen, where modern gold light fixtures hang over a twelve-foot island topped in waterfalling quartz. To the left is a grand fireplace, set into the same white quartz as the island, but this slab rockets from the floor to the ceiling.

An abstract painting in differing shades of reds, golds, and ivories hangs in the middle of it, drawing the eye to its large, violent brushstrokes.

Intricate pieces of modern art stand atop pedestals throughout the room, making me wonder how carefully everyone must have to tiptoe around them in fear of knocking one over, and a real eighteen-foot pine tree resides in the far corner, decorated in the same red-gold-ivory motif. The taste is impeccable, every single detail of this room dripping with excess, so that if the seamless glass walls weren't someone's first clue, there'd be no doubting that the people who live here are extremely well off, but the entire effect is cold. Sterile. Like walking into a museum instead of a home.

August watches me taking it all in. He has this look on his face like he's afraid I'm going to bolt. I squeeze his hand, reassuring him.

Sophie clears her throat.

August glances up at her, his jaw hardening. "Sophie. We need to—"

"Where the hell have you been?" Atticus Harker's voice thunders down the hall to our left. "You missed your meeting!"

Sophie grins at August.

He glares back at her before putting his hands in his pockets and turning toward his father. "I was with Mom."

"Don't you worry, I'll be dealing with her later." Atticus barrels down on us, a wall of Italian leather and expensive suit fabric. "You both knew how many strings I had to pull to get you this interview."

August glares at him. "And I already told you I didn't want it."

"I don't give a *damn* what you want."

August throws his arm out in front of me, protecting me from the verbal onslaught. He doesn't do the same for

Sophie, who is still standing there, shaking her head at August like a disapproving mother might shake her head at her child.

"Dad, please," he says, taking a step back and turning toward the main room, his hand brushing my hip as he turns me with him. "We have company. We can talk about this later—"

"We're talking about this now."

Atticus's hand lashes out, grabbing August's collar and pulling him toward the hall. I take an instinctive step forward, but August shakes his head at me. So I just stand there, frozen, my toes curling and my heart hammering against my chest, as his father bullies him down the hall. August gives me a reassuring smile before turning his back on me, but his eyes are haunted and his shoulders are already crumpling as if he's trying to make himself smaller, to take up less room, to be less of a disappointment, and I can see him disappearing—the boy I love—replaced by a ghost I barely recognize.

"I'll be back soon," he says over his shoulder before his dad heaves him into an interior room off the hall. I take a step forward and see what looks like a library before Mr. Harker slams the door shut.

My entire body is coiled, every muscle and fiber and sinew of my being begging me to follow him, to make sure he's all right, to keep him safe, but I have a feeling that would only make things worse. I turn to Sophie instead, thinking maybe she'll know what to do, but she just loops her arm through mine like nothing out of the ordinary is happening.

"Come on," she says. "Let's go have a chat while we wait for them to finish up."

Wait for them to finish up. As if they're playing a game of cards. As if August's father didn't just verbally attack him out of nowhere.

She leads me down the same hall. I strain to hear August's conversation with his dad as we pass by the door they disappeared into, but their voices are muffled, and all I catch are "interview" and "selfish" and "When are you going to grow up?"

Sophie clucks her tongue at me. She's already halfway up the staircase, which was designed to look as if it is floating in midair, with no banister to hold onto for support. Reluctantly, I move away from the door and follow her.

"Where are we going?" I ask as I glance through the wall of glass to my left. I was right about the helipad in the side yard. There's also a regulation lacrosse field set up along the border of the trees—presumably for August to practice on—and a garden that looks like something from the palace of Versailles.

"You'll see."

The Christmas lights bedecking the exterior of the house give us just enough light to see by as we make our way upstairs, golden pools dripping through the window and spilling onto the steps. Halfway up, I start to get dizzy with no banister to hold onto and my ballet flats slap hard ebony wood with every step, sounding so clumsy next to Sophie's softly clicking heels.

I hate how inferior it makes me feel.

We pass the second-floor landing and keep going up. Once we reach the third floor, Sophie walks down the hall and into a bedroom. It's an interior room, not on the far end of the third floor, so only the wall opposite the door is all glass, looking out over a balcony and a private pool covered for the winter. The walls on either side of us are painted a dark gray, with a black headboard on a queen-sized bed to our left and a glass desk next to a skinny black bookcase to our right. The attached bathroom is completely done in the same white quartz as the kitchen island, with a new bar of hand soap still wrapped in plastic on top of a matching white quartz dish and towels perfectly folded on an open shelf across from the shower.

"Is this the guest room or something?" I ask.

Sophie arches a brow. "This is August's room."

I stare at her.

She sits in his desk chair, crossing one long leg over the other. "Not what you were expecting?"

I shake my head. I don't know what I was expecting, but it wasn't this. There is none of August's warmth here. None of his joyful energy. I glance at the bookcase, my eyes scanning the titles written in gold lettering across black-leather bindings: *Cases on Criminal Law*, *Constitutional Law*, *Law of Torts*, *Modern Criminal Procedures*, *Cases on Property*, *Zoline on Federal Appellate Jurisdiction and Procedure*.

"This can't be his room. It doesn't look like anyone even lives here."

"I know," Sophie says. "They do have a maid, of course, so that could explain some of it, but still. Sometimes I think he doesn't have a single hobby or interest outside of school and studying law. And me, of course." She tosses her hair, as if this last part didn't really need to be stated.

Romantic comedies, I think. *He likes romantic comedies. And cooking. And sports movies. And sleeping in.*

"He lives like a monk," Sophie continues, leaning back and inspecting her perfectly manicured fingernails. "I've never even seen a single sock on his floor, and I've been here nearly every day for the past year."

Her tone is pointed. She's letting me know she's been here, and I haven't. Trying to make me feel like I don't know a thing about him, while she knows everything.

"That's funny," I say, "because I've been spending a lot of time with August too, and considering his love for empty water bottles, I figured there'd be at least a half dozen in here."

"That's where the maid comes in."

"Ah."

Sophie narrows her eyes, studying me. "I know what you're doing."

"What do you mean?"

"Please. You're not the first girl who's tried to steal him away from me, and you won't be the last."

"I'm not trying to steal anything from you."

She laughs. "Oh, Isla. You're such a terrible liar."

Something about the way she looks at me makes me feel like a rabbit caught in a viper's nest.

My gaze flicks to the open door. "We should go. August is probably looking for us."

"Don't bother. They'll be at it for a while." She holds her fingernails up to the light. "I'd be pissed if I was his dad too. He called in a lot of favors to get August that interview. I can't believe he blew it off."

My brain is shouting at me to ignore her, to go downstairs and refuse to let her draw me in. But the August I know is romantic comedies and thousand-watt smiles and laughing in the rain. He is clever and philosophical, hilarious and joyful. But the August she knows is the one I only see in undercurrents, the one molded by expectation and heartache and pain.

I am desperate to know the August that Sophie knows.

"What was the interview for?" I ask, my quiet voice echoing through the nearly empty room.

"A summer internship at Yale Law. It's usually reserved for senior undergrads, but Mr. Harker thought that if he could get August in early, he would finally buckle down and get excited about law school." She rolls her eyes. "I don't know why August fights it so much. Both of our fathers are lawyers, and they make a killing." She gestures to the room we're standing in as proof of that.

"Because making money isn't everything," I cross my arms. "Do any of you even care that he doesn't want to be a lawyer?"

"Hmm, that's an interesting comment, coming from a girl who doesn't know the first thing about him."

I narrow my eyes. "I know enough."

"Then, tell me, O Wise One, what do you think August should do with his life? What is the great career path that would be better than what his dad is offering him?"

I grit my teeth—don't say it, don't say it, *don't*—but her smile is so smug, and her tone is so venomous that the words fly out of my mouth before I can stop them. "He wants to go to culinary school, and you would know that if *you* knew anything about him."

"Culinary school?" She laughs. "August can't cook."

"Yes, he can." My fingernails bite into my palms. "He's been taking lessons at aeliana."

Sophie arches a brow. "Has he really?"

Crap.

I clamp my mouth shut and stare at the floor. "Yes, but... don't tell anyone. August isn't ready for his parents to know."

She twirls back and forth in the chair, shaking her head. "It's cute, the fact that you think you know so much about what August needs, but the truth is he couldn't go a day without the expensive clothes and the luxury cars and the hired help. He's going to join his father's firm, and do you know why?" The chair squeaks as she pushes off it, slinking toward me. Every ounce of the fairy is gone, replaced by coiled edges that slither and arch. "Because August and I are going to get married someday, and I refuse to shop in some bargain-basement-reject aisle just because he decided to get a job that pays him absolutely nothing." She walks around me, inspecting my secondhand clothes. "And he knows it too. I have too many guys salivating over me to settle for anything less."

I glare at her. "Maybe you should do both of you a favor then and leave August now, if all you really care about is the lifestyle he could give you."

"You'd like that, wouldn't you? But the funny thing is, you don't seem to get what you are to him." She shakes her head. "Girls like you come and go. You're distractions—reasons for him to put off the future he knows is inevitable. He may be planning on dumping me tonight, but he'll grow bored of you just like he has with all the others." She laughs, a harsh sound. "You'll be gone before the month is through."

23

He'll grow bored of you just like he has with all the others.
There have been others?

Sophie heads back downstairs first, while I just stand there, frozen, in the middle of a room that supposedly belongs to August even though it looks like no one has slept in it in years.

I can't believe I told her about aeliana.

Please God, no matter what she says or how she acts, let her at least care enough about August to not say anything to his parents.

Mr. Harker is just coming out of the room he took August into when my ballet flats hit the base of the stairs. I can see through the open door that the room is the library August had mentioned, with each wall stacked from floor to ceiling with leather-bound books. August comes out behind him, his shoulders slumped, his eyes distant, registering nothing.

I reach out, my fingertips grazing his arm.

"Hey."

He flinches.

And then his eyes widen, recognizing me.

"Isla."

He wraps his arms around me and nuzzles his face against my neck. I hold him just as tightly as he holds me, like we're the only things keeping each other afloat, but there are cracks in my heart now that he can't see, fissures erupting and bending and breaking.

Have there really been others? Am I just one girl in a long line of temporary distractions?

I tell myself Sophie's lying. That even if there were others, this is different. But I don't know this August, the one who lives inside these cold walls, who has been so desperately seeking a way to escape. Is that really all I've been to him? A passing fancy? A plaything to keep himself from getting too bored?

He says he doesn't want this life, but maybe Sophie's right. Maybe on some subconscious level, he realizes he couldn't live without it, so he goes through the motions of rejecting it, all the while knowing it'll get him in the end. Maybe that's why he hasn't broken up with her yet. Because for all the things he said to me in that changing room, when it comes down to it, he would rather have something fake that the world applauds than work to hold onto something real.

"I don't want to be him," August murmurs against my sweater, and it takes me a second to realize he means his dad.

"Then don't be." I swallow. "Sophie told me about the meeting. The one you were supposed to go to today."

"Sophie talked to you?"

I nod into his shoulder, breathing in that smell of teakwood and orange blossom and expensive car leather that now perfumes my skin.

He pulls away. "What did she say?"

My fingers itch to pull him back. "She was just trying to scare me. She said that I—well, that *you*—"

I try to find the words, but he looks like he's two seconds away from shattering, and somehow, I know this isn't the right time to ask how he really feels about me, with his girlfriend in the next room and his father fuming and his mother humming something in the kitchen while making herself a martini.

"It doesn't matter," I tell him.

He opens his mouth, questions burning in his eyes, but Mrs. Harker interrupts him.

"Come on, kids," she calls as she raises the martini glass to her lips. "Time to eat."

When we get to the table, Sophie is already sitting there, still playing the part of dutiful girlfriend, as if we didn't just have a conversation about how she knows August wants to break up with her.

"Oh, there you are, Isla. I was wondering where you got off to." Sophie's lips twist, something bright and unnerving burning in her eyes. "Snooping around?"

I glare at her. "I was checking on August."

"Why?" Mr. Harker asks, unbuttoning his suit jacket as he takes his seat at the head of the table. "Is he upset about something?"

August grits his teeth. "No, sir."

Mr. Harker stares at him a second longer before taking his napkin off his plate and laying it across his lap.

Mrs. Harker takes the seat on the opposite end of the table, and I realize as Mom sits down that there are only two seats left, one across from the other. There's no way I'm sitting next to Sophie, which means August is going to sit next to her and eat dinner with her as if she's still his girlfriend.

Which she technically still is.

He'll grow bored of you just like he has with all the others.

And what will happen after that? Will Sophie be his girlfriend again? Is she the constant, and the rest of us are just variables floating by? Who is the *real* August? The one who calls me at midnight and texts me all day and gives me miniature temples to remember him by, or the one who cares so much about what his father thinks—what they *all* think—that he won't break up with his girlfriend even though she's terrible, and who won't tell his family that he wants to be a chef, even though the kitchen is so clearly the only place he wants to be?

I'm starting to think I don't know August at all, and a sick, cruel part of me wishes he would just break up with Sophie here, now, in front of everybody.

He doesn't want to humiliate her, a voice whispers in the back of my mind. *He's kinder than that.*

For the first time ever, I wish he wasn't.

I take the seat next to Mom, a sinking feeling pulling at my gut.

August mouths "Sorry" to me from across the table.

I try to swallow down the knot lodged in my throat.

We start with a salad course. Mr. Harker asks Mom questions about the wedding budget and whether we're staying on track, which prompts Mom to run out to the car to grab Kathleen's binder so he can have exact figures and receipts. By the time she gets back, Sophie is telling Mrs. Harker about how she's already narrowed down her dress options for the prom because it's never too early to start thinking about it. And then she has the *gall* to ask Mrs. Harker if she thinks August should wear the same color tie as her dress or go for a complementary color. And all the while, August is just sitting there, all hard lines and clenched jaw, his knuckles white around his silverware.

Say something, I silently beg him. *Anything.*

"Claire wants all of the cheerleaders to rent a party bus

to take to the prom together," Sophie keeps going, either completely oblivious or simply not caring about the fact that August has started shaking. "But I told them that's *so* twenty years ago. I'm thinking we'll take Daddy's Bentley. Or maybe the Royce. What do you think?"

She directs this last question to Mrs. Harker, but before she can speak, August's fork clatters against his plate, making us all jump.

"We're not going to the prom together," he tells her.

Sophie hesitates, then breaks into a laugh that sounds like falling glass. "Don't be silly. Of course, we are."

"No. We're not."

She narrows her eyes. "August."

"Are you really going to make me do this here?"

Sophie glares at him, then pokes at the remains of her salad. "This was excellent." She looks right at August. "Did you make it?"

He pales.

Oh no.

Oh no, oh no, oh no.

Sophie's smile is wicked, and I have to think of something to say to fix this, to stop her from saying what I know she's going to say, but it's like watching a train wreck. My entire body is frozen. My mind is numb. I can't move—can't speak—can't think. Somewhere inside of me a voice is screaming, *STOP*, as August's entire body tenses and his eyes slide slowly, unbelievingly, to me, but the word doesn't make its way to my lips.

Mrs. Harker chuckles. "What a silly thing to say. Armando made it."

"It's not that silly," Sophie says, her fork tines scraping the gold inlay on her bone china plate. "He's been taking all of those lessons from Caio. You know, at aeliana?" Her smile grows as she turns to me. "He's really good, from what I understand."

Mr. Harker slams his fist on the table.

Mom reaches for my hand, silently communicating that no wedding is worth this much drama, and I can tell by her posture that if things get any worse, we're leaving, their million-dollar budget be damned. I squeeze her hand back, hoping she realizes I can't leave, not when August is sitting there, looking like he's half a second away from crumbling into a pile of dust.

Mr. Harker takes a swig of his wine and wipes his mouth with his napkin, as if trying to compose himself, before throwing it down again.

"August," he says, standing and buttoning his suit jacket once more. "A word?"

24

∗∗∗

The shouting is terrible. Even through the library's sound-proofed door, their muffled yells echo down the hall and into the dining space. I can't tell what they're saying, but every time Mr. Harker shouts, he sounds so furious that I bolt up, ready to run in and defend August, but Mom grabs my arm, holding me back.

"We should go," Mom tells Mrs. Harker.

"Nonsense," she replies, waving us both back down as she swallows the rest of her martini. "We haven't even had the main course yet."

"It's fine," Mom reassures her. "We'll pick up something on the way home."

"WHERE ARE YOU GOING?" Mr. Harker roars as the library door slams open. Keys jingle in August's hand. "DON'T YOU DARE LEAVE THIS HOUSE."

August strides for the front door, wrenching it open and storming through, not even bothering to shut it behind him.

Mr. Harker reappears, glancing from the door to the dining table and back again. His sense of decorum must win out because he smooths his hair into place and walks back to his seat.

"Sophie," he says, calmly. "Maybe you should...?"

Sophie rolls her eyes and begrudgingly scoots back her chair.

"Don't bother," I tell her, pulling out of Mom's grip and running for the door.

I nearly trip down the stairs and onto the gravel drive, I'm running so fast.

August is already opening his car door.

"August, wait!"

He hesitates.

I want to run around the car to him. Want to wrap my arms around him and kiss his temple, his cheek, his neck, his lips. Want to hold the shattering pieces of him until he can find a way to put himself back together.

But the look on his face stops me cold.

"How could you?" he asks.

"I'm sorry." My breath catches in my throat. "Sophie was saying all of these really horrible things about you, about how she wouldn't marry you if you didn't have a seven-figure salary and how she didn't know why you fought going to law school so much, and I just wanted—"

"What, Isla?" he shouts. "What did you want? *To rat me out?*"

I shake my head. "No. I wanted her to see you. The *real* you." My heart is thumping in my ears and my mouth is dry and all I can think is: *Please God, make him stop looking at me like that.*

"They should all see the real you, August," I tell him. "You're amazing."

He scoffs. "Yeah, well, you got your wish, and the one

thing my dad didn't scream at me was how *amazing* I am."

"August, please. You don't understand. Sophie was—"

He walks around the car, stopping right in front of me. "I don't give a *damn* what Sophie said. She's always been very upfront about who she is and what she expects out of life. But you—" He shakes his head. "You betrayed me, Isla."

Oh God. How do I fix this?

I *have* to fix this.

"Please, just let me explain—"

"I thought you were different from Sophie, but it turns out you're just like her." Disgust twists his features. "All you think about is yourself."

He walks away from me, and I can feel it happening, my heart being ripped out of my chest, but I push the pain aside and let the anger—comforting in its intensity—flood me instead.

"You're not mad at me," I shout as I charge forward. "You're mad at your dad and at yourself and at the world, but not at me."

He turns around. We're standing in front of the hood of his car, the headlights spotlighting us and stretching our shadows into a grotesque mimicry of our fight down the gravel drive.

He grits his teeth. "You don't know a thing about me."

"I know that you turned into a shadow of yourself the second you entered that house," I spit out. "I know that you live a double life, terrified of becoming like your father and even more terrified of disappointing him. I know that you dream of a better life but when it comes down to it, you're too scared to do anything to actually make it come true."

"I didn't grow up in a house like yours, Isla," he growls. "The love my parents give me has always been conditional. If I do what I'm supposed to do—if I become who they want me to become—*then* they'll love me. But anytime I make a mistake, anytime I step out of line, they turn their backs on me. Do you even have a clue what that's like? To be a child who feels like his parents will only love him if he does everything perfectly?" He shakes his head. "It's so clear your mom would love you no matter what, but I don't know that kind of security, so for you to judge me so harshly, for you to act like choosing between my dreams and my family is so easy—that's really messed up."

"You're right. I don't know what your life is like." I take another step forward, my chin up, daring him to defy me. "But I do know that you can't move forward until you decide what matters more: your calling, or your family's good graces."

"Stop."

But I can't stop. I can see him shutting himself off from me, closing every door. Everything I've ever wanted is slipping through my fingers, and even as my heart is flickering, an ember dying, begging me to fix this, to reignite, to *live*, those same words spoken in Sophie's venomous voice— *Girls like you come and go. You're distractions. Reasons for him to put off the future he knows is inevitable. He'll grow bored of you just like he has with all the others*—runs on a loop in my head as I drive in the final nail of all we could have been if only we hadn't come from two completely different worlds.

"I am *nothing* like Sophie," I tell him, "and maybe that's why you're using this to push me away because, deep down, you've already decided to do it. You've already decided to live the life your father wants you to live." I take a deep, shuddering breath, shaking my head as I stare up at him. "You say you don't want to be like him, but you already are. Too scared to cut off ties and follow your passion because you don't want to live without all of this." I raise my arms, gesturing at the six-car garage and the mansion made of glass and steel. "Well, congratulations. You are your father's son."

"Isla." He clenches his key fob in his fist. "Get out of my way."

"Gladly."

I turn on my heel and walk away from him, only flinching slightly as his car door slams shut behind me. The engine revs, and his tires peel down the drive, tiny rocks flying into the air behind him as his car disappears into the trees.

I try to tell myself it's okay, that he was never the person I was going to spend the rest of my life with. He's Frank, the guy who had an obsession with typewriters in *You've Got Mail* and who kept Meg Ryan company until Tom Hanks stepped into her life. He's Joe, the boyfriend who seemed right for Sally until she realized Harry was her real soul mate all along.

August is the placeholder, the bad breakup, the boy who never should've been more than a friend, and a million other rom-com stereotypes that describe the guy the heroine dates *before* her real Prince Charming comes along.

But this isn't a movie, and it feels like my soul has been ripped out of my chest.

I've never felt so cold.

25

***

The calendar changes from November to December. Christmas music plays from every outdoor speaker around town, telling me to have myself a merry little Christmas as I drive from school to the office and home again. White twinkle lights swirl up lampposts, and cardinals alight on ice-crusted pines, pops of red on crystal branches. Shoppers huddle together with their enormous bags, seeking the golden warmth of stores and hot cocoa and cinnamon-scented diffusers sprinkled among magical decorations.

It's been almost two weeks since our fight—the rehearsal dinner is tomorrow, and the wedding the day after that—and August hasn't called. He hasn't texted either. My heart nearly leaps out of my chest every time a text dings or my ringer goes off, but it's not him.

It's never him.

Mom and I have been frantically pulling together the last-minute details for Kathleen's wedding, and she and Mrs.

Harker have even come by the office a few times to double check everything, but August doesn't come with them. More than once, both women give me a sympathetic look, like they know I was hoping to see him, but they don't know why he's staying away. They both apologize for the fight we witnessed, but that's it. Mom takes it in stride, going into full-on professional mode. We have a job to do, and I take my cues from her, doing my best to focus on the work instead of on the giant hole August has punched through the center of my heart.

The nights are the worst. I would give anything to hear his voice again, along with the rush of his breath against the receiver when he finds something funny or the echo of his laughter rumbling through my ear, warming me from the inside out. I wonder if not talking is killing him too or if Sophie was right. If I was just a fun distraction. A brief escape from the destiny he refuses to reject.

Evelyn and Savannah take turns calling me every day. Both of them agree that I was an idiot for letting Sophie get under my skin in the first place, but they also think August was the bigger idiot for blaming me even though I did nothing but praise him—even if I did kind of, sort of, break his trust.

"That's the worst part," I tell them both on a joint Face-Time call, my eyes red, my cheeks splotchy, a dozen tear-stained tissues piled up next to me. "I can't even be mad at him because he's right. I didn't keep his secret. I made his life a living hell all because I couldn't keep my big mouth shut."

"Yeah, you spilled his secret," Evelyn says, "but he was way out of line comparing you to Sophie."

"And taking all of his anger out on you instead of on the people who have been trying to control him his entire life," Savannah adds.

"At least you only have to see him for the rehearsal and

the wedding," Evelyn tells me, "and then he'll be out of your life forever."

Forever.

"Thanks, guys," I tell them, even though that one word breaks my heart all over again. "You're the best."

I act like talking to them helped, even though I know none of this would be happening if I hadn't let Sophie get to me. August would have broken up with Sophie that night, and we'd be dating now. He'd still be calling me every night to watch romantic comedies, and we'd be seeking out every possible chance to be together.

I would still be his, and he would still be mine.

I played right into Sophie's hands, and while I'm sure August will go on and have an amazing life, only thinking of me now and then whenever a rom-com pops up on TV, I will be forever changed, looking for hints of him in every boy I date. Longing for someone to come along and erase him completely.

∗∗∗

My heels click across the marble floor of the sanctuary, echoing all the way up to the cathedral ceiling rising in gilded, star-painted arcs above me. Mom and I haven't been here, to Holy Family Church, since November, when we first toured it with the Harkers, and it's even more beautiful than I imagined it could be. Pine trees of various sizes huddle on either side of the altar, with the shortest in the front and the tallest in the back, all decked out in bright-red bows and golden twinkle lights. The very air is hushed, reverent, even as the florist and his team work on setting up the evergreen arches that will tunnel down the length of the aisle. A few bridesmaids and groomsmen have already arrived for the rehearsal, and they're all just standing around, chatting in the vestibule at the front of the church.

I try not to look for him. Try to focus on placing lanterns along the aisle and going over the music with the string quartet, but I stop short as I remember August telling his sister to go with Pachelbel's Canon over Vivaldi's "Winter" for the bridal party's entrance, the dull ache in my chest growing sharper with the memory.

None of it works. The second he enters the sanctuary, I feel him. I don't even have to turn around to know he's standing by the doors, one hand in his pocket, looking handsome and perfect and unattainable as ever.

What I'm not prepared for—what literally punches the air from my lungs when I finally turn around—is seeing Sophie next to him, wearing a slinky red dress with a split up the side that almost reaches her hip, her hand in his hand and her head on his shoulder. She spots me and smiles, then turns her head to whisper something in August's ear through red-stained lips. He looks down at the floor and nods.

He didn't break up with her. Even after what she did.

All this time I thought Sophie was lying, that she was just trying to get under my skin. But after everything she's done—everything she's put him through—they're still together, and I'm the odd one out.

I think I'm going to be sick.

I try to breathe through it. Try to focus on placing more lanterns around the sanctuary. I put some on the steps leading to the altar, in front of where the bridesmaids and groomsmen will stand, and hang others from hooks along the side aisles, behind the ornate Corinthian columns lining the nave. Mom asks me to light them so we can see if we'll need more, and as each wick catches flame, the whole sanctuary is shot through with pinpricks of stardust from the candles and shafts of pink-and-indigo light from the setting sun.

It looks like something from a renaissance painting—a dream crafted by artists that in no way could ever actually exist on earth, and yet here it is, a slice of otherworldly beauty and glory, as if a veil has been torn apart from the world we know to reveal the actual world hidden underneath. Mom and I share a look, a knowing—*this* is why we do what we do. For moments like these.

And then, even though I know I shouldn't, even though I know I'm better off acting like he doesn't exist, I search for August.

I watch him walking down the aisle with one of the bridesmaids. Watch him standing on the steps leading to the altar. Watch him laughing about something with the other groomsmen (his polite laugh, not his real one, and the fact that I know the difference makes my heart ache even more).

And every time I find him, he finds me too.

He's always the first to look away.

I beg Mom to leave me out of the rehearsal dinner, telling her I'll stay at the church and make sure all the flower arrangements are accounted for, but she says she'll need the extra pair of eyes at the restaurant, since rehearsal dinners are notorious for drunk, out-of-town uncles making scenes. It'll be my job to keep an eye on the number of drinks each person has while Daphne oversees the food and Mom orchestrates the flow of everything else.

Halfway through dinner, Mom catches me staring at August and Sophie. At her hand on his hand. At the fact that he's not pulling it away.

She puts her arm around me. "You okay?"

I shake my head.

Mom wipes the tears from my eyes and, kindly, *gently*, reminds me that August is the client, along with the rest of his family. It's the wedding planner's creed that no matter how involved our feelings may become, the weddings we coordinate are never about us. We have a job to do, and we can't let anything get in the way of that.

"But when this is over," she says, pushing my hair behind my ears, "we're going to get a giant tub of ice cream and an even bigger box of tissues and watch every sappy, romantic movie you want to watch until you start to feel better."

"What if I still don't feel better by Monday?"

Mom sighs. "Well, you've already caught up on all that work you missed when you were sick. I don't think one extra day at home will hurt anything."

I sniffle. "Thanks, Mom."

I don't look at August or Sophie for the rest of the night. And when everyone finally leaves and it's just Mom and me combing through the room, making sure no one left anything behind, all I can think is: *One more day.*

One more day, and August Harker and Sophie Calloway can run off and live their perfect country-club lives together, and I can start to forget about the boy who gave me racing through the rain and the Temple of Dendur and chicken soup and stolen kisses and desperate promises in a closed-off changing room.

And someday, if I'm lucky, I'll be able to watch romantic comedies again without thinking of him, and it will almost be like he never existed at all.

26

***

A layer of freshly fallen snow greets us when we pull up to the church the next day a full four hours before the ceremony is set to begin. It dusts the front courtyard like powdered sugar, fringing the evergreen garland that wraps around the iron banister on either side of the stone staircase. It's so beautiful, I don't even mind shoveling the steps and laying down salt as Mom works on bringing extra weather mats into the front vestibule, especially since areas around Richmond experienced a torrential downpour and even some flash flooding just a few days ago, and Mom and I are both thankful no damage was done to either the church or the reception site.

Kathleen and her bridal party arrive an hour before the guests are due. They squeal and giggle and tease Kathleen about how to make her husband happy on his wedding night as they change into their dresses. I help a bridesmaid bobby pin a broken strap on her dress and

give another double-sided tape for the gap at her bust-
line. I also apply a touch of stain remover along a coffee splotch on red silk heels and offer Kathleen a Q-tip
dipped in Vaseline so her burgundy lipstick won't smear
onto her teeth.

The groomsmen arrive on a party bus as I'm lighting
the candles. August is with them, wearing his cross-country sweats, his hair slicked back, his tuxedo bag held casually over his shoulder.

I finish lighting the last lanterns in the center aisle
and stand.

His eyes lock on mine.

Breathe...

He takes a step toward me, opening his mouth like he
wants to say something, but then his future brother-in-
law is slapping him on the back and guiding him toward
the groom's chamber, and whatever he wanted to say has
been forgotten, lost in a flurry of guffawing groomsmen and
sneakers squeaking across sacred tile and Daphne telling
them they really must be getting dressed now.

The guests arrive twenty minutes later. I help the ushers
guide them to the side aisles so as not to disturb the evergreen archways and lanterns in the center. It takes over an
hour, but we manage to pack five hundred people into the
enormous sanctuary by five o'clock on the dot, just in time
for the ceremony to begin.

Sophie arrives last, taking a seat in the front row, where
Mrs. Harker will also be seated after she's escorted in by one
of the ushers, and where Mr. Harker will join them after
walking Kathleen down the aisle. Sophie smirks at me, brow
arched. Every square inch of her face is painted to look like
a siren's song—same red lips as last night, perfectly lined
brows, smoky eyeshadow that makes her look twenty-five
instead of seventeen.

I pretend I don't see her.

Kathleen's fiancé enters the sanctuary, with August and the other groomsmen following behind, taking their proper places along the stairs leading to the altar. My breath catches as August faces forward and his eyes latch on mine again, but this time, I look away before he can.

It's almost over, I remind myself. *Six more hours and he'll be out of your life for good.*

It's supposed to be a comforting thought, but my heart is crumpling in on itself just like the water bottles August loves to twist.

Pachelbel's Canon rises joyfully into the air as the setting sun casts a rose-gold glow through the stained-glass windows. The candles strewn throughout the room push back the encroaching darkness, and I know from last night that the pink-and-indigo shafts of light will come next, like God Himself is celebrating this union along with the rest of us.

I don't think I've ever seen anything more magical in my entire life.

The bridesmaids walk down the aisle carrying bouquets of holly, ivy, evergreen needles, and red poinsettias mixed with cream-colored roses, each of them wearing a different style dress in the same scarlet silk. They line up on the opposite side of the stairs from the groomsmen. Once the maid of honor, Kathleen's best friend from college, takes her place at the top of the stairs, the music switches to the wedding march, the familiar notes echoing across the cathedral ceiling, and then the sanctuary doors open and Mr. Harker and Kathleen step out.

This is the moment when everyone turns to get their first glimpse of the bride and when I turn to look at the groom. I love to see the awe and the joy flash across his face as his bride walks toward him. Love to witness the tears streaming down his face as he thinks about how lucky he is to have found the woman he wants to spend the rest of his life with.

But this time, when my eyes should be finding Kathleen's husband-to-be, they trail toward August, and my breath catches in my throat, because he's staring right back at me.

27

* * *

The second the ceremony concludes, I jump into my car and race to the conservatory to see if Daphne needs any help setting up the reception space in the Glass Room or the cocktail hour in the Rainforest Room. Mom stays behind at the church with the bridal party, both so she can be on hand if there are any problems during their photo session and so she can keep everything moving on schedule, a particularly difficult task when everyone and their mother wants a solo picture with the bride and groom.

I keep myself busy throughout cocktail hour, making sure the waiters continue circulating the room in the preferred clockwise rotation, counting drinks of specific guests I was told to pay close attention to, and helping other guests locate the bathrooms in the lobby. I also check on the reception space, but it turns out there was no need. Daphne did a fantastic job. Everything is exactly as it should be, from the centerpieces to the spacing of the tables to the chocolate favors for the guests. The Christmas trees look just as stunning as the conservatory promised they would—like standing in the middle of an evergreen forest—and the stage has been erected on the north side of the room, where the swing band is already tuning their instruments while, outside, the full moon plays peekaboo behind silver-rimmed clouds the color of dark-blue velvet.

Once the reception begins, our job tends to get easier. It's mostly just keeping an eye on things at this point, making sure everything is running smoothly. I usually cherish this time when I can sit back and enjoy watching the vision we've been crafting for the past year—or, in this case, the past six and a half weeks—unfold. But tonight, I hate it, because my eyes keep drifting back to August, sitting at the bridal table with Sophie next to him as his date. She's rubbing his back and leaning on his shoulder and taking pictures of the two of them with her phone.

Everything inside me hurts.

I would think the fact that he looks so miserable would give me some tiny morsel of joy, but it doesn't, because all it does is make me think, *Why?*

Why are you still with her?

My traitorous brain starts listing all of the possible reasons—because she looks like a supermodel, because she's social-media famous, because she's the kind of girl I could never be no matter how hard I try—until my head swims and my stomach twists.

Air.

I need air.

I stumble out of the reception just as the dancing begins and send up a silent prayer of thanks that Mom's too busy corralling the groomsmen (who are currently trying to scale one of the trees in the Rainforest Room) to notice me leaving.

I wend my way through different rooms—Desert, Meadow, Everglades, the Orchid House—not even paying attention to where I'm going. I push through foliage reaching onto stone pathways, past tropical pink flowers bigger than my head, and skirt around burbling fountains and placid ponds. I walk and walk and walk, telling myself to calm down, but it feels like the whole world is pressing against my chest.

The weight is unbearable.

I take a turn and almost hit my head on an archway made of volcanic rock.

You know, the reception is going to be at night. And I checked the lunar calendar. It's going to be a full moon.

I take a step forward.

So, how about it? Want to sneak away with me that night and check them out?

The archway opens up.

We'll make our escape when everyone's distracted.

The room is awash in the pale glow of moonlight, filtering in silver strips around a break in the clouds and down through the glass ceiling above me. The small blue, purple, and green spotlights are also lit, so that stepping from the archway onto the cobblestone path has the effect of walking into a supernova. Every single one of the moonflowers has opened, reflecting the glow of the moon here, the lilac or the ocean blue or the neon green of a spotlight there. The waterfall crashes and the bridge creaks, and it's like walking into a fairy garden crafted just for me.

The tears come hot and fast as I stop in the middle of the bridge, my mind racing through every late-night phone call, every conversation, every slide of his palm against mine.

The bridge creaks behind me.

"I told you I'd be the one in the tux."

August.

The top two buttons of his shirt are undone, the sleeves rolled up to his elbows, the fabric a bit rumpled. His jacket and tie are gone, left on the chair where I saw him place them as soon as he sat down, and he has his hands in his pockets in that catalog way that I love so much. He's trying to sound like he's teasing, but he looks so anguished, like his heart is being ripped out of his chest, that the nonchalance of his words falls flat.

He swallows. "I was hoping I'd find you here."

I wipe the tears from my cheeks.

"Where's Sophie?" I ask, my voice croaky and awful.

"Probably calling her mom to come pick her up." The bridge creaks again. "Or hitting on one of my cousins, maybe."

"Why would she be doing that?"

He ducks his head as he takes another step. "Because I just broke up with her."

Everything inside of me slows. Did he really just say what I think he said? I try to wrap my head around it, to grasp the hope that is clinging to his words, but it is a small, brittle, flickering thing, and the only word my brain can form is: "Why?"

"When you told me I was stuck—that I couldn't move forward until I figured out what mattered to me—you were right. About Sophie, about culinary school, about every-thing." His jaw tightens as he looks at me. "Isla." His voice breaks on my name. "I'm so sorry. For what I said. For what I did. I have no excuse other than the fact that I'm a total bumbling idiot who doesn't deserve your forgiveness, but I'm hoping I'll get it anyway."

My heart thumps in my chest at the words I've been so longing to hear, but I'm just so tired—tired of loving a boy who doesn't know what he wants, of hoping and praying and losing and crying—that his apology pings off a mental wall I hadn't even realized I'd built, but I'm thankful for the protection it provides me, for the way it cuts me off from him and from all the ways I know he could hurt me.

So instead of jumping into his arms and letting everything go as I might've done the night we fought, I lean against the bridge, assessing him.

"As of last night, I was still the enemy," I say. "What changed?"

August moves to the railing opposite me, hands still in his pockets, the waterfall at his back.

"I was mad that you told Sophie about my lessons with Caio. My dad was screaming at me and banging his fist on his desk and raising it like he wanted to hit me too. I couldn't think straight. And then after..." He clears his throat. "I knew Sophie was the one to blame, but I didn't break up with her then for the same reason I hadn't broken up with her before—because she was my father's choice, and I just so desperately wanted him to look at me like he wasn't disgusted by the sight of me—" He stops. "But then I was moving through that reception, shaking the hands of the same clients and the same partners from my dad's firm that I shake at every Christmas party, hearing them go on and on about how I'm going to make a real shark of a lawyer someday, and Sophie was taking another selfie and replying to all of the comments on her page, getting annoyed with everyone and everything around her, and I just knew...no matter how badly I want my father's approval, I can't do this for the rest of my life. It's killing me."

"So, you broke up with Sophie?"

He shakes his head. "First, I told my father and his entire board of directors that I'm not going to Yale next fall; I'm going to whatever culinary school will take me, and I'm going to become a head chef at an incredible restaurant. And *then* I broke up with Sophie." He glances down at the boards beneath his feet. "I'm just sorry it's taken me so long to do it. I should've told my dad that years ago, and I should've broken up with Sophie the minute I knew I was falling in love with you."

"And when was that?"

"The second I met you."

I laugh, a strangled, hiccup-y sound. "The first time we met, I shouted 'Hello' in your face like I'd never met another human being before."

"It was the cutest hello I've ever heard."

"You hurt me, August."

"I know."

I cross my arms over my chest, blocking him out. "I was fine before I met you, you know. A little too in love with love, maybe—a hopeless romantic who couldn't wait to find someone—but I wouldn't have been in such a rush to fall in love if I'd known that finding someone would turn my whole world upside down. That I would have trouble sleeping if I didn't hear your voice on the other end of the phone before I went to bed. That I would crave your smile and your laughter and the sound of those stupid water bottles crinkling in your hands. I didn't *need* those things before I met you, August, but now they're all I can think about, and I hate you for that. For swooping into my life and wrecking everything and leaving the second it got hard."

"Well, that's where we're different," he says, "because I *wasn't* fine before I met you, Isla. It was like I was drowning in slow motion. I was surrounded by people who didn't understand what my problem was, and the only ally I had—the only person in my family who ever stood up for me—was leaving for London. And then I met you." He pushes off the railing. "I've never met anyone who can pull me out of myself the way you can. Out of my circumstances, out of my doubts, out of my fears, out of everything my parents have made my life to be and see me for who I really am." He inches forward, looking up at me from beneath those lashes that make my heart stop every time I look at them. "Isla, being with you—it was like finally coming home. And the past two weeks without you have been the worst weeks of my life." He pulls my hands from the railing. Presses his forehead against mine as he closes his eyes. "I know I don't deserve it—I know I don't deserve you—but I'm begging you. Please. Forgive me."

His hands feel so good shielding mine. So strong. So secure. The ice around my heart is melting, and I can feel myself opening up to him. I try to fight it—try to hold on to all my self-righteous anger and the wall my mind has built to protect me—but suddenly all I want to do is step into his embrace. Bury my face in his neck. Breathe in that scent that has been haunting my dreams, always out of reach.

But I don't do any of these things. Instead, one word falls from my lips.

"No."

He tenses. "No?"

I shake my head.

A single tear escapes his lashes. He takes a deep breath, then kisses the backs of my hands and murmurs, "I understand." He pushes my hair back one last time and stares at me a moment longer, as if trying to memorize every line and curve and angle of my face. "Goodbye, Isla."

He turns to go.

"I can't forgive you," I say, my voice stopping him, "until I know you've forgiven me too."

He glances back at me, a question in his eyes.

"I should have never told Sophie your secret," I explain. "You trusted me with something that was so special to you, and I shared it with someone I knew couldn't keep it. I am the worst person in the entire world—way worse than Sophie."

He shakes his head, crossing to me and taking my hands again. "No, Isla."

I look away from him.

"I'm *glad* you told her. I wouldn't have had the courage to finally stand up for myself if you hadn't." He cups my chin, gently turning my gaze back to him. "Losing you was the worst thing that's ever happened to me—do you hear me? It felt like half of my soul had been ripped out of my chest. I never want to feel that way again."

I half laugh, half whimper. "Me neither."

"Please. Forgive me. Be my girlfriend. Make me the happiest man in the universe. And I promise I will spend every day of the rest of my life trying to be worthy of you."

"August?"

"Isla?"

I glance up at him. At his steel-gray eyes and the joy that is surging in them. At the purple-tinted mist rising from the waterfall in opaque swirls behind him. At his hair cascading over his brow as he stares down at me, looking at me in a room full of magic and moonflowers and starlight as if *I* am the most beautiful thing here.

"Kiss me?"

He smiles—his brightest one yet—before crushing his lips against mine. His hands are on the sides of my face, in my hair, around my back, and I meet the desperation of his kiss with the ferocity of my own. He is teakwood and orange blossoms and leather, champagne and chocolate and mint sorbet, and I could kiss him for a thousand years and never get enough.

August.

My August.

If falling in love with me has been like coming home for him, it's been like waking from a deep sleep for me, and there is so much I don't know about what our futures will look like, but I do know this: whatever we do, wherever we go, I don't want to lose the person I am when I'm with him.

August Harker is my One True Love, my Happily Ever After, the Joe Fox to my Kathleen Kelly, the Harry to my Sally, and there's a reason people like Nora Ephron and Nancy Meyers write about true love in a world that so often ignores it or acts like it's all fairytale nonsense: because when you find that person who makes your heart sing, who seems as if they were specifically made to fit into the crook of your side, to complement your weaknesses with their strengths, to bring out the stars in your eyes and lift you higher than you ever thought you could go, someone has to tell you how special that is. Someone has to remind you to never let that go. Because that's where the magic really is. It's not in the epic proposal or in the perfectly planned wedding or in the tropical honeymoon—it's in the cherishing, in the recognizing, in the never forgetting that one day you were stumbling through this world and the next you were flying, all because that one special person walked into your life.

And as we stand here on this bridge, August's arms wrapped around me, moonlight and flowers the color of gemstones and crashing water surrounding us, I vow to never forget this moment—how our two worlds collided and aligned and exploded into a universe of us. I don't know what's coming next, but as long as August is by my side, I can't wait to find out.

And judging by the way he nuzzles against me, whispering my name like a prayer, oblivious to the faint sounds of five hundred people toasting and dancing and drinking just a few rooms away, adoring me with his words and with his lips and with his eyes, I know August feels exactly the same way.

A Look At:
All I Want For Christmas is
the girl who can't love

Get swept up in this holiday romance as Chelsea Bobulski's All I Want for Christmas young-adult contemporary series comes to an end by exploring the hope and magic of unforgettable love.

College freshman Savannah Mason doesn't believe in magic or true love. She believes in science, and science tells her that love is nothing more than a biological impulse to breed—an impulse that can, thankfully, be ignored. Which is a good thing because no woman in her family has ever been lucky in love. In fact, all of them have ended up broken hearted and insistent on blaming a mysterious, vengeful curse. But Savannah is determined to rewrite her story, and as far as she's concerned, she's never going to fall in love.

Jordan Merrick is a junior at William & Mary and on the fast track to obtaining his life's goal: becoming the next Ron Chernow. He vaguely imagines that, someday, he'll have a wife and kids. But like Hamilton himself, Jordan's drive is to accomplish his goals as quickly as possible. Love can come another day once his career is cemented.

What neither Savannah nor Jordan planned on is meeting each other, and as they keep crossing paths on campus and Savannah finds herself helping at Jordan's archaeology site, all their reasons for putting their love lives on the back burner start to blur.

Forged together, Savannah and Jordan investigate Savannah's family's curse on love and explore a collection of love letters between a revolutionary soldier and the girl he left behind. But when they come face-to-face with the truth about themselves—and with the truth about what they've become to each other—Jordan's outlook on love starts to waver, and he begins to wonder if he can convince Savannah that love is real. But will Savannah run before her heart is able to let go of cynicism and believe in the power and magic of love?

At once thought-provoking and charming, All I Want for Christmas is the Girl Who Can't Love will stir a longing in every reader's heart for the hope in magic and romance that can only be found during the holiday season.

AVAILABLE DECEMBER 2021

Acknowledgements

***

This was SUCH a fun book to write, and I have so many people to thank for it!

First, I am so thankful to God for everything about this book. From the first book seeds to the finished product, He went alongside me, encouraging me and inspiring me and, oftentimes, downloading scenes so quickly into my brain that my fingers couldn't even move quickly enough across the keys to capture it all. What a joy-filled and beautiful experience writing this book has been. It has truly been a journey I will treasure for the rest of my life.

I am also so thankful to Rachel Del Grosso and the entire team at Wise Wolf Books for giving me the opportunity to write this book and for cheering it on and championing it. I feel so blessed to be a part of a community that really believes in the power of getting just the right book into a readers' hands at just the right moment, and it is my sincerest hope that this book will find its readers and be a beacon of light and joy to those who need it most. Thank you for giving this book (and this series!) the opportunity to do just that, and for helping to make this book the best it can possibly be.

I am forever grateful to my agent, Andrea Somberg, for always going above and beyond in supporting me and my writing. You're always there for me whenever I need it—I couldn't ask for a better agent!

Thank you to my parents, for instilling in me from a young age the belief that I could do anything I put my mind to. These books would not exist if it weren't for your encouraging my love for storytelling and teaching me how to work hard and know that good things follow self-discipline (along with teaching me how to enjoy and appreciate the really important things in life, a theme that often finds its way into my books).

Thank you to Jane for your tireless efforts in holding down the fort at home during my writing days so that this book could do exactly what it wanted to do the entire time I was writing it: fly from my fingertips to the page.

Thank you to Nathan for being my person for the past seventeen years. I've said it before and I'll say it a thousand times more: every single couple I write is inspired by you, and by all the different ways we've grown together. Despite what many may think, you absolutely can find your soulmate in high school (which is exactly why I write about it!) and you are most definitely mine. My love for you is eternal, my gratitude everlasting.

Thank you to Emerson and Caleb for taking me out of my writing cave for all sorts of whimsical adventures, enchanted playtimes, and wonderous nature walks. Seeing the world through your eyes will never stop being magical. Mommy loves you so much.

Thank you to Nora Ephron and Nancy Meyers, and to all of the other incredible screenwriters and authors who have brought some of the most memorable romantic couples to the big screen, the small screen, and the creaking spines of beloved paperbacks. I loved getting to share my enthusiasm for your work through August and Isla. Thank you for writing and producing stories that lighten hearts while simultaneously imparting ancient wisdom about relationships and human interaction, and the importance of knowing and being known. You are all complete and utter Rock Stars.

And thank you to my readers—I pray this book will be just as enjoyable for you to read as it was for me to write. I am so grateful for each and every one of you, for the notes you send, for the excitement you share, and for the kinship we possess as fellow book lovers. May your lives be filled with strong coffee or comforting tea, crackling fireplaces, warm blankets, and beautiful stories that companion you throughout your own magical journeys.

About the Author

Chelsea Bobulski is a graduate of The Ohio State University with a degree in history, although she spent more of her class time writing stories than she should probably admit. Autumn is her favorite time of the year, thanks to college football, falling leaves, cozy fireplaces, and the countdown to the most magical holiday of them all: Christmas. She is the author of *The Wood* (2017) and *Remember Me* (2019). She grew up in Columbus, Ohio, but now resides in northwest Ohio with her husband, two children, and one very emotive German Shepherd/Lab mix.

CPSIA information can be obtained
at www.ICGtesting.com
Printed in the USA
LVHW041614021221
705095LV00014B/2301